OUTSIDE WITH
ELEPHANTS

Collin,

You are such
an inspiration for me
+ has

I hope you enjoy the read!

With love,

[signature]

OUTSIDE WITH ELEPHANTS

A NOVEL

BY MARTIN ANGUS, JR.

NEW DEGREE PRESS

OUTSIDE WITH ELEPHANTS

A Novel

ISBN   978-1-64137-959-5   *Paperback*

978-1-64137-781-2   *Kindle Ebook*

978-1-64137-782-9   *Ebook*

For Enid, Pearl, and Madge.

TABLE OF CONTENTS

ACKNOWLEDGMENTS

Writing a book has been a long-standing ambition of mine, and one I have been afraid to actualize. If it weren't for the consistent love, belief, and support of my family and friends—many of whom are depicted in this tale—this would not have been possible. Thank you for being there.

When setting out on a long journey you've never embarked on before, you never know how much work it will take to reach your final destination. I've discovered along my journey writing *Outside With Elephants* that publishing a novel takes a village.

Thank you to Professor Eric Koester for creating a platform for aspiring writers to believe they can accomplish such a feat.

Thank you to my editors Brian Bies, Kristy Carter, and Cass Lauer, for being so patient with me as I procrastinated month after month with chapter submissions. You are an incredible group of editors, and I am so grateful for your patience.

And thank you to everyone who gave me their time for a personal interview, pre-ordered the eBook, paperback, and multiple copies to make publishing possible. You all helped spread the word about *Outside With Elephants* and ultimately helped me publish a book I am proud of. I am sincerely grateful for all of your support:

Adam Radice
Alex Santana
Alfred Lockhart
Andre Belgrave
Andrew Dolny
Andrew French
Anthony Battaglia
Anthony Buntin
Anthony Roden
Ben Hirsch
Chid Liberty
Christina Myrick
Christine Peterson
Collin J Newton
Connor Enright
Constance M. Sterner
Cristian Hidalgo
Cuba Flowers
Dane Holt
Daniel Dormer
Daniel Modic
Daniel Riggle
Danielle Angus
Deric Cahill
Enid Angus

Eric Sulizter
Erica Eleam
Erick Muse
Eve Matthew
Fidelia Schnarr
Frank Lewis
Gamal Breedy
Garrett Kincaid
Gioconda Chiera
Glenda Estrada
Imani Davis
Jacob Messimer
Jake Balbes
Jasmin Begovic
Jocelyne Correia
John Radvany
Josh Sefrin
Juliano Pereira
Justin Sefrin
Kane Nerys
Kerry Lynch
Kevin Bodniza
Krista Carr
Krista Ramroop
Lane Vrba
Leonila Capron
Lou Redmond
Malika Eure
Manuel Morgan
Marc Weisi
Martin Angus, Sr.
Martin Rafla

Matthew Rodney
Megan M. Clifford
Mike Muniz
Nadine Saxton
Natasha Souza
Nathalie Perdomo
Nicole Picon
Niko Gkionis
Olawole Isijola
Paul Killian
Randall Ledet, Jr.
Shawn Gordon
Sofia Bodniza
Stephanie Argast
Stephen Portee
Steven Moschetti
Tiandra C. Jones
Tiara Solomon
Tim Coyne
Valerie Curry
Vershima & Aondongu Tivzenda
Vincent Picone
Wendell T. Joseph
Wesley Nicholls
Zubair Ahmad

PART I:

ELEMENTARY

HILLCREST - FRANKLIN, SPRING 1998

11:27 A.M.

A peculiar calm ran through the halls of Hillcrest Elementary—an unusual tranquility this close to lunchtime. Golden stars filled with the names of honor students on orange and brown construction paper cut into the shape of stenciled turkeys lined the tiled walls. The awkward smile of a pre-pubescent overachiever taped under a plaque reading *Student of the Month* hung boastfully in the entrance of the old, one-story building.

On this particular day, I found myself gallivanting through the hallways. I had told my teacher, Ms. Lyman, I was going to the bathroom, but I just wanted to roam. After having successfully misled her, my dopamine levels were off the charts. I was free. Free to be and do as I pleased. Free to dance, hum, sing, and think. *What am I gonna do with all this freedom? Should I go to the bathroom and just hang out? Sit under the stairs? Drink water from the fountain for a long time and walk slowly back to the classroom?* As I weighed my options, I spotted a smaller, younger, fair-skinned boy drinking at the water fountain down the hall.

Perfect. I shook my hands at my sides and cracked my knuckles as I approached him. *He's little. This will be easy.* There was silence. I stood over the smaller boy until he stopped drinking. He looked up at me.

"Move, you little third-grade pussy," I demanded.

The frail, flush-faced boy didn't flinch. He just looked at me and narrowed his eyebrows, as if looking through me. I stared back. There was no way I was going to break his stare. After what felt like an hour, he broke the silence.

"Fuck you," he said plainly and returned to drinking from the fountain.

Whoa.

Surprised by the interaction, I stood there and watched the smaller boy drink for a few moments. *This little guy.* I smiled to myself. I was at least a foot taller than this kid, and he'd just spoken *down* to me. I weighed my options. *Do I punch him? Nah, he's too small, and I don't want to get in trouble. Do I push him out of the way and start drinking water? Eh, he might start to push back and start a fight, and I don't want to get in trouble.* I decided to shrug it off, and slowly headed back to class. As I walked away, a deep feeling of accomplishment came over me, as if I had got what I was looking for, but couldn't quite put my finger on what that was.

Walking away satisfied, I continued humming and dancing.

"This...is...it...Everything I've dreamed of..."

Sliding my feet along the old hallways, I soon arrived back at the door of the classroom. Upon reaching the door, I paused, took a deep breath, and entered casually.

2:21 P.M.

When school let out, the front of Hillcrest Elementary was an orchestra of movement. Droves of kids spilled out of the building, many forming groups circled together on or near the grass. Some wore backpacks slung over one shoulder; some dragged their bags on the ground.

On this day, at our spot near the buses, I found my three friends: Chad Normandy, Patrick Green, and Elio Ramirez. When I emerged from the building, Chad was the first to catch my eye.

Back then, I felt that Chad and I were pretty similar. We were just about the same height, the same complexion, and he had an older brother the same age as my older sister. When you're nine, you don't need much more than that to think you're similar.

Deep down, Chad and I weren't that compatible, and our relationship wasn't very deep. What kept me gravitating to him was his uncanny resemblance to my cousin Adrian. Man, there wasn't *anyone* in the world I looked up to more than my cousin Adrian, but we'll get to that later. On that day, though, as I walked up to the group, they were already deep in discussion—if you want to call it that.

"C'mon, man. Derrick is selling slice pops ten for a dollar, and you selling them shits for like *twice* as much. You a whack dealer, dog," Chad shouted.

"Yeah, but Derrick don't got grape, watermelon, or peach— and I do. So, like I said, seven for a dollar, three for fifty cents.

Take it or leave it, fucker," Elio replied. Elio loved calling people "fucker."

"Man, you're crazy!" Chad shouted back. "Whatever, yo. Yours prolly got pocket lint on 'em anyway."

"You just mad you not getting a discount," said Elio.

As I got closer to the group, Patrick was the first to notice me. He always was. "What's up, Martin?" Patrick asked, smiling.

Patrick Green was one of the nicest kids I had ever met up to that point, and when you're nine, it's hard to tell what to do with the nice ones. If you were too kind, you could be perceived as weak or afraid. I know different now, but we couldn't be sure back then.

Patrick was different, though. We knew he wasn't weak. He felt like that cool cousin who came into town for Thanksgiving and would play fight with you, but you knew they wouldn't really hurt you so you never got mad when they pinned you down. He was like a prince who had arrived in a foreign land, only to uplift the townspeople and show them their true worth. He had a small, mirthful mouth and smooth coiled hair that rested peacefully atop an always warm face. He stood sturdily with a centralized grace that complemented his positive disposition. I liked Patrick; we all did.

Patrick was the newest member of the group. He'd transferred from a neighboring town about two months into the school year—which usually would put a target on your back, but everyone took a liking to him immediately. He was athletic, kind, excelled in class, and went out of his way to make sure everyone felt seen. Surprisingly, none of my friends were jealous of him. At least, not that I knew of.

"'Sup, Pat," I replied coolly. It could sound like a question, but it was how we said "hi."

Naturally, Patrick replied with a touch of laughter, "Man, these guys are crazy."

Elio continued, "Look, I know you're a hungry little boy, so I will help you out. If you kiss my shoe, I'll give you a discount."

Elio had moved into town a few years back from the Dominican Republic and had a pretty strong accent when he spoke. While Chad, Patrick, and I were nine, Elio was eleven and significantly bigger than the three of us. He was supposed to be in sixth grade but had remained in the fifth grade for not having passed his reading requirements. Something about Elio didn't sit well with me. He always had this smirk on his face, as if he knew something no one else knew. Like he could sense a certain weakness in people—and knew how to exploit it. Simply put, I didn't trust him and was kind of afraid of him.

I didn't extend or expect any greeting from Chad or Elio, and I didn't get one. They were far too invested in their dispute.

"I don't need a discount from you! I'll just hit Derrick, or Thomas, or Ashley. The principal probably sells 'em cheaper than you!" Chad responded, pointing in Elio's face.

Patrick and I laughed a lot at that one.

"Good one, fucker," Elio replied.

Elio then reached out and grabbed Chad's collar just above the strap of his backpack and mushed his head around as Chad desperately tried to wiggle out of his grasp. There was no use, Elio was too big, too strong.

"Get off me, man. Ew! You smell like goose crap!" Chad screamed.

Patrick and I laughed even louder.

As much as I was entertained by Chad and Elio fighting over cost per lollipop, there was only one reason I would hang out by the buses. I scanned a group of classmates standing near the third bus from the back. *Nope, not there.*

My eyes began sorting through a group of girls huddled under the oak tree out in front of Ms. Kirkland's classroom. *Nope, not there.*

I was beginning to get anxious. I knew that any minute now, Mr. Hoagland was going to yell for everyone to get on the buses, and I was definitely *not* going to get on the bus before I saw her. *Boom. There.* Bianca Pelham.

Whenever I saw her, everyone and everything else would come to a halt—instantly demoted to deep insignificance. Hunger? What's that? Laughter? Only if she was laughing too. Crime? Not in mine and Bianca's world.

To be fair, I'd had small crushes in my boyhood before Bianca. In fact, my favorite thing about school was knowing that my crush would be there. In preschool, my parents claimed Bridgette Laney was my "girlfriend" because our parents teamed up to dress the two of us up as Jasmine and Aladdin one Halloween. In second grade, I admired Sofia Bodniza because she wouldn't stand in line when Ms. Fryer said, "Single file!" and for the one time she spit in the water fountain on the way back to class from lunch. Or even Samantha Portee, who used to give the bus driver the middle finger in the rear-view mirror in the mornings. Yeah, Samantha was badass. But *no one* was like Bianca Pelham.

Bianca was sweet. She had these big, honest green eyes with a splash of orange. When I looked into them, it felt like I was looking into the universe. It was as if she laughed more than she spoke. Can laughter be a language? If so, that's what she spoke. She most often wore her hair in big tight braids, with barrettes tied at the end that always matched her outfits. One time during lunch, she laughed so hard at something one of her friends had said that she knocked heads with the person sitting behind her. First, she turned to make sure the other person was okay, and when she saw that he was, she grabbed her own head and started to cry. I wanted to get up and help her, but I knew I couldn't. It wouldn't make any sense. I was so far away from her.

She was the most beautiful thing I'd ever seen. Whenever I laid eyes on her, a caged dove was set free at the top of a mountain in Ireland, and a caterpillar would unfurl its wings. The roar of bus engines would transform into hundreds of humming stallions, awaiting my commanding whistle to trot the two of us—my queen and me—into a gradient abyss. The only problem was Bianca didn't feel the same. I'm not even sure she knew who I was.

My fantasy that day was abruptly halted by a scurrying second-grader bumping into me as he rushed to his mom's car. *C'mon, fool!* The stallions returned to buses, maggots became moths, and Bianca didn't know I existed. Great.

"Okay, everyone, get on the buses or begin walking home!" Mr. Hoagland eventually shouted.

Dang. "Aight, y'all. I'm out. Peace, peace, peace," I said to the group, rushing to get on my bus before the doors shut.

"Bye, Martin, see you tomorrow," Patrick responded. Chad and Elio didn't even notice.

As usual, I was the last to enter the bus, and of course, I headed straight for the back, where the cool kids sat. However, on my way to the rear, I saw a familiar face sitting alone in a three-seater, staring out the window. A small round head, fair skin, and slick dark hair. The third-grader from the water fountain.

I stood for a second, waiting for the fair-skinned boy to notice me. He did not.

I blurted, "Yo."

With stern eyebrows, the small fair-skinned boy slowly took his eyes off what he was looking at out the window and stared up at me, maintaining his stoicism. He stared at me almost as if he didn't recognize me. "Yo," he said in his high-pitched, eight-year-old voice.

The bus pulled away from the curb, launching me into the seat with the fair-skinned boy. After clutching my books to make sure I didn't drop anything, I started the conversation: "What's your name anyway?"

"Kane," he responded, still stern.

"You look Spanish. You from Spain?" I asked.

"No, are you?" he responded, returning the challenge.

"No," I said matter-of-factly. "I'm from Jamaica. You ever heard of it?"

He paused. "Yeah, it's in the Caribbean."

It wasn't what Kane was saying that impressed me. I could care less that he knew Jamaica was in the Caribbean. It was that he wasn't afraid of me. He wasn't afraid to look in my eyes and reject me—and even insult me. I wasn't sure what I was looking for that day, but I knew I'd found it in Kane.

After a few seconds of silence, Kane asked with little warning, "You wanna come to my house and play basketball?"

"Yeah," I replied with no hesitation.

And we sat in silence until the bus slowed down for Kane's stop.

KANE'S HOUSE

When the bus pulled up to Kane's stop, I scrambled to grab my bag. *Wow, that's a nice-ass house.* I shuffled out my seat and down the steps of the bus.

Kane's house was a sprawling renovated two-story, mid-century family home that stood about thirty yards off the street. It had bright beige siding with freshly painted brown shutters framing three large clear windows, allowing you to see directly into the house. The driveway was long with newly laid cement and lined with sunflowers, rosemary plants, and fern bushes. On both sides, tall bougainvilleas in full bloom stood sentry like something out of a fairy tale.

As we walked farther along the driveway, a woman emerged from the house.

"Hi, Mom, this is Martin. He's on my bus and lives up the street. Can we please play some basketball?"

Kane's mom didn't respond right away but, instead, stared at him a lot like the way Kane had stared at me. Like she didn't recognize him or something. *Hmph.*

After stroking his hair, she leaned in close to me and extended her right hand. "Well, hi, Mr. Martin. Nice to meet you."

I looked up at her. She had long, dark, shiny straight hair that seemingly reached the ground. She had the bluest eyes—bluer than any I'd ever seen—and her skin was porcelain white with dimples carved into each cheek, gentle wrinkles near the sides of her mouth.

She looks so nice. I slowly removed my right hand from my pocket to reached out for hers. *Does she like me?*

"My name is Connie, but you can call me Ms. Connie," she said.

"Hi, Ms. Connie. I'm Martin," I said.

"You have such beautiful eyes!" she replied.

Okay, She likes me. "Thank you," I said, beginning to blush.

"And such a beautiful smile!"

She really likes me. "Thank you."

Kane rolled his eyes.

"Well, I know you didn't come here to talk to me. It's just fine for you to play basketball in the driveway so long as your parents know that you are here. Kane, go on into the garage and show Mr. Martin the phone to call his parents."

Kane and I took off running to the garage where he pointed to a phone hanging on a wall just near the door. "Here you go," Kane said. "Ask your mom if you can stay. I'll be dribbling."

As I reached for the receiver, I noticed three shiny bicycles hanging upside down from the ceiling on two large hooks, fleece pullovers on smaller bronzed industrial hooks, and what looked like work boots in handmade wooden cubbies just below the bikes. Three sets of skis hung parallel against a polished wooden beam, just above a large bin filled with toys and well-used sporting equipment. In a low corner, I spotted a small refrigerator, a stereo system just above it, and countless tools, paints, and well-crafted artifacts meticulously placed along the back wall.

None of the brand names meant anything to me at the time, just indicated that the objects were new, but it was all so neat and carefully placed. *Damn. This place is clean.*

When I called home that day, I knew my mom wouldn't answer. She didn't get home from work until six and it was only around three o'clock, so when I called it was my cousin Lisa who picked up. Lisa, my mother's sister's daughter, and her two young sons lived with my mother, my two sisters, and me in our three-bedroom townhouse.

I wasn't too fond of Lisa because she made me do chores all the time, but we'll get to that later. What mattered more to me was that my mom enjoyed having Lisa around because Lisa was a bit older than we kids, and provided my mom with an adult companion. That didn't keep me from giving her some attitude, though. When you're a kid, attitude and mischief are all you have.

After getting off the phone with Lisa, I ran into the driveway and began to play basketball with Kane.

Kane was the first to shoot the ball, scoring his first shot. "Respects," he said.

"What does that mean?" I asked.

"It means, whenever someone makes a shot, the other person has to run after the ball and bring it back to them."

Makes sense. I went after the ball and gave it back to Kane. He shot it a second time from the same spot and made it. Again, I retrieved the ball and passed it to Kane. He then shot the ball a third time and made it. Again, I honored his "Respects."

"Okay, now let's play. Check-up," Kane said.

"Let's go," I said confidently. I was ready to get his ass.

Kane passed me the ball, and I passed it right back to him. He faked right, then dribbled left, and took an off-balance shot. It went in. *Nice move.*

"One to zero. Winner's ball!"

We checked the ball up again. This time, I wasn't going to let Kane get the best of me. He tried to do the same move, but this time, I stole the ball. I then dribbled back to the middle of the driveway, faked left, faked right, then took a shot from long distance. I missed.

Shit. I immediately sprinted to the bottom of the basket and grabbed the rebound using my height to lay the ball in over Kane's head.

"One to one. Winner's ball! Check." I said, proudly. Kane looked at me with a scowl as he passed the ball back to me, firmly.

I faked left, faked right, and drove past him to the hoop again for an easy lay-up. "Two to one. Check."

I then did the same move and scored. I was on a roll. "Three. Check."

While I was filled with adrenaline and excitement to be winning, Kane, on the other hand, was getting upset. "Stop doing the same fucking move," he barked. "Why don't you take a shot?" It was much more a demand than a question.

"Let's play soccer now," he eventually said, dismissing basketball entirely.

He grabbed a pair of cleats from the garage and marched into the backyard, where he took off his shoes. I rolled the basketball into the garage, picked up the soccer ball, and jogged over to keep up with him.

Kane's backyard was long and beautiful, surrounded by bushes of beautiful flowers and nearly-perfect grass with a back deck that ran the total length of the house. Bees flew from flower to flower and birds flew in and out of the birdhouse nestled beside the shed near the trampoline.

We made our way over to low-laying deck steps and took a seat. Kane began putting on his cleats.

"Those are pretty cool," I said.

"Yeah; they are called Predator Precisions. They're the best. Feel 'em. It's kangaroo leather."

"Shit, that's sick."

"Yeah. The best players in the world use these cleats, like David Beckham, Zidane, and Luis Figo."

I had no idea who he was talking about, but I nodded along anyway.

"Alright, Let's do this," Kane demanded.

After he finished tying his cleats, he stood up, grabbed the ball, and began to juggle. Now, I was familiar with the sport of soccer, but I certainly wasn't good—and here's this kid with some shiny ass new cleats and a big backyard with birds and bees and shit. I was out of my element.

Kane passed me the ball and back-peddled as if to create space between us. I bit down on my lip and tried to control the ball, but it went under my right foot and rolled beyond me, finally stopping against a fence a few yards away. After retrieving the ball, I faced Kane to pass the ball back to him. I awkwardly approached the ball head-on using my toe to send it back in Kane's direction, but it went drastically off the mark.

After we played this way for a few hours, Ms. Connie walked into the backyard. "Alright Mr. Martin, it's getting dark. Do you live nearby?"

"Yes, I can walk home from here, just a few blocks."

"Alrighty, well, it was very nice to meet you, but you should be heading home now, I don't want your mother to worry."

"Thank you, nice to meet you too," I said, looking at the grass and then up at Kane. "Bye, Kane."

Kane looked at his mom and then back at me. "Peace," and he ran through the garage and into the house.

HOME

I lived in a small community, about a mile away from Kane's house, at the end of a cul-de-sac.

My house was the house with all of the bikes in front. And in the backyard, my older sister, Terri, would be chillin' with her friends, smoking cigarettes, and free-styling. I was incredibly impressionable at that age and looked up to no one more than my older sister and her friends. From their baggy jeans to their "couldn't-care-less" attitudes, it was safe to say there was always something happening at my house.

That night I walked into our household's liveliness, as always. Terri and her friends were in the backyard smoking and laughing. Lisa and her sons were in the living room watching

TV, and my other sister, Danielle, was on the computer play-ing *Sims*.

The house was moderately messy, not disrespectfully, but there were many things out of place.

I said a quick, "Wassup," to everybody and headed upstairs to my room. For the first time in my life, I had my own room. My mother felt middle school age was too old for a young boy and young girl to room together, so she put my two sisters together in one room and allowed me to have my own.

I threw my stuff down, sat on my bed, and turned on my Nintendo 64 just to unwind—but then stopped. I had sneak-ers out of place in my closet, shirts on the floor, cups on my dresser, and a karate trophy laying on the floor behind my door. All I could think of was Kane's garage and its neatness. Not just how neat it was, but how *nice* it felt. I wanted to feel that way again, so I spent the next two hours cleaning my room. I vacuumed, wiped down my desk, and lined my sneakers up neatly in the closet.

As I was pulling a bunch of ancient papers from deep in the closet, I found my old laptop. I decided I'd break it open and record something silly.

"It's ya boy, Lova Chocolate, and we're here on radio 7-0-5, bringing you stupid cuts…yeah." I then slid my fingers slowly around the edges of the laptop. "Tell me how you like it, I'll tell you how it is."

From downstairs, Lisa exclaimed, "Martin! You need to come do these dishes!"

I rolled my eyes and tried to continue recording, but I knew Lisa wouldn't stop yelling until I did my chores.

"I love my woman, and I love my homies...Yeah, I love em... Whoop whoop...We're here jazzing out...vibing...giving you the hits you lo—"

Lisa yelled, "Martin! Where you at? Come down here and do these damn dishes!"

Shit.

Reluctantly, I stopped recording, grunted, and made my way downstairs.

SOCCER - FRANKLIN, FALL 1999

Every day after school for those next six months, my routine had been the same. I would hang around with Chad, Patrick, and Elio, trying to catch a glimpse of Bianca Pelham before Mr. Hoagland shouted us onto buses. Once on the bus, I would join Kane in the same three-seater to see what kind of mischief we could conjure up. Kane would usually do whatever designated deed, as I looked on in admiration.

Kane was something else. I couldn't quite understand how someone so small and unassuming could be so cunning, deceiving, and brave. He always had something to prove—and he did so successfully.

Fortunately for us, there was also some productivity sprinkled in amongst our mischief. We spent a lot of time together playing in the backyard. When summer arrived, we would throw a football and jump on the trampoline but more often than not, we would play soccer.

"Hey, Martin, try this," Kane said one day as he jumped off the trampoline and onto the grass. He made his way over to the deck and grabbed the soccer ball. I sat up on the trampoline, watching.

He used the bottom of his foot to pull the ball toward him, then proceeded to scoop the ball with his toes until it balanced perfectly on the top of his foot.

"Can you do this?" he shouted.

"I don't know, man. Never done anything like that!" I shouted back.

"Come try!"

So I went. I hopped off the trampoline, heading in Kane's direction. When I arrived, the ball was in his hands.

"Alright, so you want to break it down into segments. First, master the balance of cradling on the top of your foot. We'll do the second part once you've got that."

I grabbed the ball from him.

"Don't worry, bro, I'm here," Kane assured me.

After a few months of this, I was getting good. Days and days spent chasing Kane around, passing the ball through each other's legs, launching long passes from one side of the house to the other, and trying to knock bottles, cans, cups, hats—whatever we could find off of the porch—with the ball from a distance, got me pretty confident in my ability to manipulate a soccer ball.

As summer came to an end, Kane was able to convince me to try out for the local soccer team. I went home and asked my mother. She agreed that it would be a good idea.

JAMAICA, SUMMER 2000

"Man, my mom is sending me to Jamaica," I said.

"Jamaica? For what?" Kane asked.

"For the rest of summer, for basketball camp. She says she wants me to learn about where I came from."

"Basketball camp? But you suck," Kane joked.

"Very funny," I said sarcastically. "Whatever, man. I don't want to go."

"Yeah, that does kind of suck."

"And she's sending me alone! For a month! What am I going to do for a month?"

"You'll be fine, yo," Kane assured me.

"Yeah, I'm sure it will change my life," I said sarcastically.

KINGSTON

When I arrived at Norman Manley International Airport in Kingston, Jamaica, it was hot. I'm talking *hot*, and I was nervous. I had been to Jamaica before, but never by myself.

The plan was for me to meet with my mother's friend, Marland Nattie, who was the president of the Jamaica Basketball Association (or JABA, for short). Marland was to meet me outside of the airport with a sign that read *Martin Jr.*, which I thought was pretty cool. I was going to have my name on one of those signs at the airport and be all-important—like a businessman.

As I exited the airport, all the chaotic movement around me was a bit overwhelming. I scanned to my right, where a short, stout woman with a pink bucket had yelled, "Ginneps, ginneps, who wan' ginneps! Right here, suh!"

A few feet behind her, a man with an open backpack was shouting, "Nextel! Nextel! Wireless! Buy one, get next one 'alf off!"

Just behind the woman and the man was a line of what looked like taxi drivers holding signs for passengers they were tasked with picking up. *Martin Jr.? Nope.*

After about ten minutes spent looking for my name on a sign, I gave up. No sign for me. The trip was starting off great. With my head hung low, I walked over to a nearby bench and sat to wait for Marland.

What am I doing here? I wish I home with my friends, man. Why did my mom think this was a good idea? Can they tell I'm American? Am I gonna get shot? Stabbed? Just keep your eyes low, you'll be good. Marland will be here, he'll find you.

Just before I really started spiraling, Marland arrived.

My first day in Jamaica, after that, was great. Marland took me to the Bob Marley Museum, to watch a local soccer game, and to eat KFC. I felt like a spoiled child, but the fun had to end at some point.

Around seven that evening, Marland dropped me off at the G.C Foster Sports College. That was where the week-long basketball camp was to take place. I was to spend a week at the camp itself and three weeks with Marland immediately afterward. After showing me my dormitory for the week, he left. That was when the loneliness set in.

Sure, my parents were Jamaican, but that was a lot different from me being in Jamaica—alone. I didn't know any of the kids there. I didn't know how to communicate with them. Could I be myself? I struggled. That night, I didn't know what to do, so I pulled out a pen and paper and wrote. First, I wrote a note to my mother letting her know how much I missed her.

Mom,

I miss you. Thank you for being such a good mom. I know you only wanted me to come to Jamaica to know more about where you come from, but I am ready to come home now. It is hot and sticky, and I don't know anyone. I love you.

MARTIN JR.

I never planned to send my mother that note, but it was therapeutic to write it. Something about putting my thoughts on paper helped me deal with the fear and uncertainty. I kept writing my thoughts.

This place is kind of scary
It is dark and everyone is loud
Will they know that I am American?
Will they make fun of me?
I'm no good at basketball
I miss my friends
I miss the way it was
Why am I even here?

I wrote at a feverish pace. Thoughts, arm, hand, fingers, pencil, paper, boom. That was it. I felt so comfortable with myself. Though externally there was little I could control, when I wrote, it was my world.

Man this kinda sucks
I feel kinda stuck
In this place I've never been
In this war I'll never win

Oh, wow. That was pretty good!

Jamaica, Jamaica, Jamaica
This land of my mom and dad
Jamaica, Jamaica, Jamaica
Why do I feel so sad?
Jamaica, Jamaica, Jamaica
Won't you fill me with your joy?
Jamaica, Jamaica, Jamaica
To you I am just a boy

I was soaring. I felt like each poem was a hug from my mother. Each rhyming couplet was a kiss on the forehead, and each word was a smile. I couldn't stop. I wouldn't stop. For the rest of my trip—though challenging—every time I was alone, I wrote another poem. By the end of the month, I had over two hundred poems about my mother, Jamaica, and my friends back home.

BACK HOME FROM JAMAICA

By the time I got home, I was three inches taller, ten pounds heavier with athletic muscle, and had fallen in love with expressing myself in verse. Being able to write through rhyme was unlike anything I had ever experienced. The confidence that came from it felt like magic. It was therapy, mixed with problem-solving, mixed with creative expression. It became everything. When I was listening to a beat that moved me, writing rhymes to it, I could create my own world and take myself there. No matter what was going on in my life situation, I had control over something. There was a place I could go.

On the day I returned, the moment I got home, I started writing Bianca a note. I wrote a poem about how I felt about her, how beautiful she had always been to me. I told her how I noticed her barrettes and her belts and how they always matched. I told her about how I would only make her smile, and how I saw chariots and angel wings when she was near. After penning the note, I stowed it into my backpack and rode my bike to Kane's. When I arrived at his house, he was laying on the trampoline in the backyard.

"Bro, come with me to put this in Bianca's mailbox," I said.

Kane looked at me, both arms at his side. "Let's go," he replied, a smile creeping across his face.

At the end of every school year, the students of Hillcrest were given a directory with everyone's address and home phone number. I used that to direct us to where Bianca lived. We rode our bikes for about forty-five minutes before arriving.

"This is it," I said.

"Great, where's the mailbox?" Kane asked.

Good question. We expected the mailbox to be on the street next to the end of her driveway, but it wasn't. After a few moments of scanning her property with our eyes, we saw that there was no mailbox, just a rectangular slot in the front door where mail could be placed.

"Just my luck, man. You've got to be kidding me!" I said.

I was petrified. I was nervous enough just putting the note in her mailbox but having to sneak up to the door and slide the letter into the house itself was a whole different ball game.

"I'll do it," Kane said confidently.

"Yeah?" I asked, unsure if he was joking or not.

"Give it to me," Kane said as he quickly snatched the letter out of my hand, dropped his bike, and ran down Bianca's driveway.

He's crazy. They're going to see him. My heart was racing.

Just as he was getting close to the house, the garage door started to open.

Oh, my god. He won't make it!

His little body got farther and farther away from me, and closer to the door. Once the garage door reached about a quarter of the way open, I saw him dash the letter into the slot on the front door, then leap off the porch into the grass on the opposite side of the house.

He did it! But I had his bike, and I was in the middle of the street, easily viewable from the house. I needed to hide. I grabbed the handlebar of Kane's bike with one hand, hopped on my bike using the other, and began riding down the street. I didn't look back. I eventually found a bush a few houses down and slid myself and the bikes behind it. Moments later, Kane caught up to me, laughing.

"Pussy," he said, with a smile on his face, catching his breath. We rode home laughing, celebrating a successful mission.

Three weeks later, on the first day of eighth grade, Bianca walked up to me in the lunchroom and kissed me on the cheek. I melted.

"Yes, I like you too," she said.

And just like that, I got my Bianca.

PART II:

HIGH SCHOOL

THE HOMIES - FRANKLIN, WINTER 2006

Kane had become my younger brother. We would spend every day after school and entire summers together. It was around sophomore year in high school, though, that I had begun hanging out with a different crowd, and acquired another sibling.

Jordan Jenkins was a smooth, charismatic, athletic specimen. He was a year older than me, but already a lifetime cooler. He stood at six-foot-one, with a bright joyful demeanor, always ready to smile his way into or out of something. I'll never forget the moment our friendship began.

I was a shy tenth grader and he was a popular eleventh grader at Franklin High, where we were both on the varsity soccer team. I was the up-and-coming sophomore workhorse out to prove something, and he was the overachieving, well-proven go-to-guy. The king of the castle and leading goal scorer. There was one time, during a game against one of our worthier rivals, North Hunterdon, we had given up three goals in the first twenty minutes. It was scorching hot outside at the tail end of dog days in late August, and our team was exhausted. We had lost five of our star players who graduated the year before, and were struggling to find synergy on the field.

At halftime, Jordan went ballistic. "Listen, boys, It's not going down like this. We are *not* going to let these motherfuckers walk all over us. Not this year, not this team." He pointed at Eric, our star midfielder. "I watched you throw-up all summer long, busting your ass up those hills." He pointed at our center defender. "You're a senior! You worked four long years to make varsity and you're here now. Are you going to let these pussies take that away from you?" I was trembling. *Point at me.* "And you…" *Oh, shit. He's pointing at me.* "You're the youngest player on this field. I watched you knock down motherfuckers twice your size! Show us you deserve to be here! We need you."

Floored.

He needs me. Say no more. When we walked out on to that field, North Hunterdon didn't know what hit them. I kept their best player scoreless, Jordan scored a hat trick, and we went on to win the game 4-3.

Jordan's talents didn't stop on the soccer field. He was also on the varsity basketball team, track team, and the "got all the women he wanted" team. Seriously, the guy was a magnet. After basketball games, there would always be a pack of freshman and sophomore girls waiting to say hi to him. When he entered the field, court, or room, people watched

him. I looked up to him, and I barely even knew him.

One day, at soccer practice, I decided to challenge Jordan. At this point in the season, we had a simple athletic working relationship. I was the starting left defender, and he was the "wherever we need you" for the team. Toward the end of our second water break, I said, "I bet you can't meg me." To *meg* someone means to dribble the ball between their legs and continue onward.

He looked at me, smirked, and accepted my challenge.

I passed him the ball and squared my feet, ready to earn his favor by successfully defending against him. He faked left, faked right, then stepped his left foot over the ball and used his trailing right heel to slide the ball between my legs. The ball never even touched me. It was smooth as butter. He looked at me, laughed, and continued to jog onto the field, signaling to the rest of the team that water break was now over. I went from being a distant admirer to actively exalting him.

Something must have clicked in him after that as well because he began to extend himself to me more. During games, he would check on me. "You good? You need some water?" Whenever I would see him in the hallways, he would always make sure to give me a head nod or dap me up. High-school was never the same after that. I was *in* now. I belonged.

Over the next two years, Jordan and I got close.

He'd invite me to parties, he'd bring me on double dates when he'd meet a new chick from a neighboring town who had a cute sister or friend. He'd pick me up in his parents' car, and we would just drive and talk about any and every-thing. Jordan had become my older brother and one of my strongest advocates.

When Jordan and I began getting close, he was already part of a friend group. They called themselves, "The Homies."

After Jordan's class graduated, I was the last of the group to still be in high school. When Jordan and the other homies came back home during their college breaks, it was on. The fact that they all wanted to hang out with me—when they could have been spending time with other college kids—made me feel special. I felt like we could go anywhere, do anything. Nothing was impossible. I felt safe with them. I felt accepted.

Jordan: *Hurry up, bro. We waiting on you.*

Me: *Coming*

When I walked out the house that night, I could see Jordan's gun-metal Acura MDX SUV in the distance.

"What's good, Martin?" Ceza said as I got closer to the SUV.

"What's good?" I replied.

"What's good?" V said.

"Chillin', ain't shit. What's up wit' y'all?" I replied, smiling.

Ceza was sitting in the MDX's seat, breaking up weed into a five-dollar bill.

"Shit, just came back from the store, finna roll up and listen to this Weezy," Ceza said.

Ceza was twenty and the oldest member of the group. He set the trends. He was the first of us to drive, he was the first to wear huge fitted hats, and he was the first to develop the bug for sneaker collecting. Ceza was generally reserved but extremely outspoken—if you were to discuss something he was interested in. The thing is, it seemed to me like he was only really interested in sneakers, hip-hop music, light-skinned girls, black and milds, weed, and school. It sounds simple, but Ceza was brilliant. He graduated with a perfect GPA and was offered a full ride to the school of his choice. He chose Morehouse College in Atlanta, Georgia.

"Apollo, where the dutches at, bro?" Ceza questioned.

"I got 'em right here," Apollo replied.

"Well, pass me them shits, man!" Ceza exclaimed.

"You are literally rolling one up right now. Relax. I promise you they aren't going anywhere," Apollo replied.

Anthony "Apollo" Apollon was a nineteen-year-old under-ground encyclopedia. He could tell you when every Hip-Hop album in the '90s was released, under what label, and how many copies sold in the first week. He could recite to you every Nike sneaker released from 1995 to 2005 and how many colorways were released. His love of counter-culture was astounding. You would think that knowing all of those things would make him a nerd or an introvert. On the con-trary, Apollo was one of those people who got along with everyone. His senior year in high school he was voted Class Clown, Best Smile, Best Dressed, *and* Most Likely to Succeed. At six-foot-two, under 200 pounds with a boyish smile and intelligent charm, it was easy to like him and even easier to learn something from him. He followed Ceza to Atlanta and attended Morehouse as well to study Marketing.

Luckily for me, Jordan ended up attending a small private university in Jersey City on a full soccer scholarship. I was pumped because I had been accepted on a partial scholarship to play soccer at Stevens Institute of Technology in Hoboken, NJ—only a few miles from Jordan's school.

While Ceza rolled up, I wanted to share with the group what I was working on inside.

"Yo, y'all wanna hear some of what I been writing?"

"Yeah, let's hear that shit," Ceza encouraged.

I cleared my throat.

"I'm bone-crushing boy, there's no discussion
Walking on the sky putting Yoda in dutches...It's nothin'
Catch the king with his duchess on sand no one touches
My brand's going nuts 'cause the demand is so disgusting"

"Fuck!" Apollo interjects.

"Peep
Get down or lay down? Well, you should go to sleep
You too scared to be prepared...too coward to creep
I turn my flavor into vapor then shower the streets
You'd rather live with gimmicks than spend an hour with beasts
"Look!

I'm Rick Ruben if the bitch is Cuban
I'm Mark Cuban if the bitch is shootin'
I'm setting picks if the six is movin'
Can't be a bitch when it gets confusin'
...Cause when you're rich, you're on a different rubric"
"

What!" Apollo exclaimed. "Nah, nah, nah, nah...What!"

"Yeah, that shit was dope," Ceza vindicated.

"Yo, what inspired the lyrics?" Apollo asked, leaning back in the passenger seat, now looking at the car's center console, with me in his periphery.

"That's a good question. Ya know, I've been feeling like an underdog recently and this was my letter to the world. That I'm a force to be reckoned with. Outside of Weezy, I'm the best rapper in the world right now. No question," I replied.

Ceza lit the first blunt and passed it to Apollo after taking a few hits. Apollo took a deep inhale, closing his eyes. The night was still. Streetlights flickered in the distance. Consistent humming from crickets gently reminded us it was summer. Light from the center console shined in our faces as clouds of smoke filled the car, neatly escaping through the tiny cracks at the top of the windows.

"I turn my flavor into vapor then shower the streets," Apollo whispered to himself in admiration.

"You need to do something with music, bro. That shit ain't normal, B," Apollo eventually said.

"Straight up, bro. You're dope," Ceza added.

"G shit," Jordan confirmed, nodding.

"You sure you wanna go to college?" Ceza joked.

I closed my eyes and smiled shyly. I didn't take compliments well. Something about them made me cautious. I perceived that when people receive a compliment, it meant they could stop trying. They got what they came for—validation. I could feel that same thing in me, that I could do that, and it scared me. Compliments scared me. My response, in that moment though, was to act in defiance to that fear.

"Turn the beat up," I demanded. *Go.*

"It's a cold-ass world, I need a jacket, a hoody or vest
I'm bulletproof—Teflon at its best
Call the press, let them know I made a hell of a mess
Out here high off the tree like a pelican's nest
Who's next? I'm chewing through competition...No opposition
Grew up with no pot to piss in, still optimistic
Apologies to the women that I forgot to visit
Don't cry over spilled milk, baby. Mop the kitchen!
We in the car like, fuck it. Stars, like fuck it.
So I'm getting high spittin' bars, like fuck it.
On a spaceship headed up to Mars like, fuck it.
Apollo 13, getting fully charged like, fuck it!"

"Oh, shit!" Apollo screamed. "What!"

"Damn, son!" Jordan shouted, accidentally ashing the half-burned blunt on his lap. "Did you write that earlier or are you making all this up right now?"

"Right now," I responded, as smoke continued to fill the car.

"Bro, that was crazy!" Jordan barked aggressively. "Like, am I buggin'? Or was that shit crazy?"

"That's what I'm sayin'," Apollo turned to me, adding, "You might actually want to reconsider college, bro."

"I already know I'm the best. My mind just goes and puts it all together. It's wild," I said

"Grew up with no pot to piss in, still optimistic. I love that," Apollo said.

"If you love him that much, just kiss him, damn," Ceza joked.

"If you jealous, just tell us, bro," Apollo snapped back.

We all laughed, but I could feel tension began to fill the car. What once felt like a hazy mission into space aboard Apollo 13 had quickly begun to feel like a car full of smoke with five fully-charged young men in it. I think Jordan felt it too because he quickly shifted the conversation.

"So what we doing next?" he asked.

"Yeah, Martin, what's good with Cocoa?" Ceza added.

I looked down at my phone. I had a message from Cocoa I had overlooked.

I'll meet you at Uche's in 15, it read.

"Aight...Let's go to McDonald's then head to Uche's. Cocoa and her homegirls are gonna meet us over there," I said.

"Dope!" Ceza shouted menacingly.

Jennifer "Cocoa" Williams was a girl I met online a year earlier. She was a year younger than me and attended a nearby high school. Cocoa had long, wavy hair, big brown eyes, and a body many would call too mature for her age. Around town, she was well known for being reckless, showing off her figure online, and social media bio taglines like "Cocoa Flames" and "Nasty Nini" garnering her a massive following of high school boys, as well as a laundry list of young women who wouldn't mind if she was never seen again.

For reasons I couldn't fully understand, Jennifer took an unhealthy attachment to me. Even though young men from all over the internet would like and comment on all of her photos, she would only like and comment on mine, saying things like *My baby* and *Damn, so fine.* One day, she showed up at Bianca's house and began banging on the door, threatening to beat her ass. It really upset Bianca and certainly annoyed me. But Cocoa knew Bianca was my long-time girlfriend and hated it.

As much as I claimed I wanted nothing to do with Cocoa, she was exciting. She brought a thrill to what would otherwise be a quiet, regular evening. I knew that anytime I hit up Cocoa, she would respond, and would gather her troops together. To her credit, she was incredibly persuasive. Every few months, Cocoa would be rolling with a new set of girls, all eager to please and prove their loyalty to her. It was rumored that while in middle school, she once made a girl shave her mother's head as she slept as proof of her loyalty to "the infamous Cocoa Flames."

Whenever someone asked her if the rumors were true, Cocoa would respond the same way—"What do you think?" or a more clever, "Would you?" Though the story was never confirmed, she was defined by stories like it, and she was well aware of it. The homies and I were, too.

Jordan put the car in drive and pulled off down the street, away from the dead-end and in the direction of McDonald's with his brothers in tow. For the five of us, every night together was a new world. One that we would dream collectively and experience holistically. Filled with THC, hormones, adrenaline, and confidence in our brotherhood, we were nirvana. Between us, we had $196.36 collectively in cash and equivalents, a group of girls who had something to prove on their way to meet up with us, and Uche's open house to hang-out in. We felt invincible.

As the loud music filled Jordan's Acura, stars shone down on us like the eyes of our ancestors smiling in approval from above. The moon's light blanketed the stillness of the night, adding to its majesty. Squirrels, I mused, were nestled in their meticulously built dens deep beneath the pine trees that decorated the curb-lined streets.

Apollo stared out the passenger-side window, contemplating the timbre and cadence of the bass versus hi-hats in the song blaring through the speakers, Ceza slid the nail of his pinky finger down the spine of a cigar, spilling its contents into a small black plastic bag, as I pressed send on my phone, letting Uche know we were en route to his house and to leave the porch light on if his mother had left for work.

UCHE'S

When Jordan pulled the MDX into the driveway, the porchlight was already on. *Dope.* Uche's house was a humble, one-story ranch with a long white fence, small driveway, and a bench in front. When we got out of the car, we found Uche waiting at the door for us. A wave of relief washed over me. We'd arrived. We were safe within the confines of Uche's house to do as we pleased. Safe from the judgment and ignorance of the outside world, and safe from the police.

I immediately went into the kitchen to grab some water, Ceza went to the couch to finish rolling blunts, and Jordan sat on the floor and stretched his legs, still feeling sore from his last college soccer game. The air in the room was calm. We felt free and unadulterated. No one to answer to—just time. It was close to eleven, and Uche's mom was a nurse so we knew she wouldn't be home until nine tomorrow morning at the earliest, giving us about nine hours to do and be as we pleased. After we finished what was left of our McDonalds, we began to establish what was next.

"Aight, so I just heard back from Cocoa. She got three friends and three bottles," I said.

"Her friends bad?" Jordan asked as he extended his arm, stretching his left leg.

"She said two of them are bad, and one is aight, but that the one who's just aight is still down for whatever," I responded.

Uche then let out a loud laugh and leaned on his piano with a big smile swept across his face. "I call one of the bad ones. Shouldn't take long!"

Ceza chimed in, "I get the other bad one, shit."

Cocoa just gonna tell them what I tell her.

"Low-key, It's up to Martin. Cocoa does whatever this nigga says. And Cocoa's homegirls do whatever Cocoa says," Jordan added.

"Well, shit, if it's up to Martin..." Uche turned to me. "Nigga, gimme the baddest one or you gotta go home."

A test.

"If I go home, Cocoa and her homegirls gon' go home, and nobody gets nothin'," I returned.

"If Cocoa and her homegirls leave, all you motherfuckers leave, and I get good sleep."

Another test.

"Nigga, chill, they not even here yet. Let's just see what's good when they pull up," Apollo said.

"I ain't even tripping, as long as they ain't annoying, I'm good just smoking and playing 2k," V added.

With us all under the age of twenty-one, we couldn't buy our own liquor and were beholden to the bottles Cocoa would bring. I wasn't concerned though. If there was one thing I knew about Cocoa, it was that if she said she was going to do something or bring something, she was going to do it, and bring it, and then some.

"Aight, she said they're 'bout five minutes away. Uche, we got anything in the fridge to mix?" I asked.

"I should have something." Uche said, as he went to the kitchen and grabbed a carton of fruit juice.

A few moments later, Cocoa texted me. *We're outside.*

Cocoa walked in first, her friends following. One of the friends was short and fair-skinned with a dimple on the left side of her face without needing to smile. Another was tall, quite beautiful, and dark-skinned, and the third friend was short with a medium build, big rosy cheeks, and a pigeon-toed stance.

"Say what's up to them," Cocoa directed her friends.

"Hi, y'all," the girls said together in awkward obedience.

Cocoa then walked up to me with puppy dog eyes, staring. "Hi, Daddy," she whispered as she reached for my hand.

"Let me get these for you," I said, grabbing the plastic bag of alcohol from her hand. I could already smell the liquor on her breath as I leaned in close.

"Tell your friends to get comfortable on the couch. I'll get the drinks together," I said.

"Y'all heard him, go chill on the couch. Me and my baby will be over here," Cocoa directed.

The air was awkward. Cocoa's friends were awaiting direction from Cocoa, and the homies were awaiting directions from me. No one quite knew how to proceed.

"Y'all drink?" Jordan asked, in his usual way of trying to make everyone feel a bit more comfortable.

"I do. I don't know about them," the medium-built, rosy-cheeked friend answered.

"I do," the other two answered in unison.

Before I could reach the dining room table to set down the bag of alcohol, Cocoa grabbed my arm. "Baby, let's go to the bathroom," she begged.

I side-eyed her, trying to gauge where she was mentally. *Is she just drunk? Is she high? How attracted to her am I right now?*

"In a little bit. Let's get everybody sorted," I replied.

"C'mon!" she demanded, whispering a little louder. "I want you, baby. I'm here. I came here for you."

"I got you. I got you. Just chill," I replied, trying to quiet her.

I then poured drinks for everyone in the room, and the festivities began. After about forty-five minutes, the mood had totally shifted—we were all laughing and zoning.

Out of nowhere, as if lightning had struck, we heard a loud knock on the door. The room went quiet.

"Who's that?" Jordan whispered.

Uche shrugged and gently walked over to the door. *Police?* Uche quietly looked through the peephole. There was no movement in the room.

"It's Bucky," he eventually said, a confused look on his face.

"Bucky?" Jordan asked.

Bucky was in eleventh grade at Franklin. None of us were particularly close with him, which made it all the more awkward that he would be knocking on Uche's door, especially so late and on a night we weren't throwing a party. Uche opened the door.

"Cez here?" Bucky asked.

"Yo, why you bangin' on my door like that for?" Uche demanded.

"Uche, man, I don't mean no disrespect to you but is Cez here?"

Uche paused. I could see the sweat quickly beginning to build on his face. "Bro, you gotta get outta here, man. I don't know what you think this is but you gotta get outta here."

One thing I knew about Uche was that he did not like to repeat himself.

"Uche, I'm sorry but I gotta know if Cez is here. This nigga came to my house last night drunk as shit ringing my doorbell all crazy, woke my mom up and when she answered the door, he knocked her down being all drunk. He got me kicked out the house, man!" Bucky's voice trembled. "I'm sorry, Uche, but I got fight him, yo. Please don't jump in."

Uche balled up his fists. "Yo, I'm sorry about what happened at your house with your mom and all that, but you're about to come to my house knocking on my door looking for somebody? What if my mom was home?"

"You be having parties, bro. We know your mom don't be home at this time. I'm sorry, yo, but I need to see Cez. We'll go down the street, bro." I could hear Bucky pacing from side to side.

When I looked over at the couch, Cocoa's friends were still, Jordan was beginning to stand up, and V was making his way over to the door.

"Yo, you heard the man, bro. Get the fuck outta here!" V shouted, as he tried to move Uche out the way. "You want to fight Cez, you gonna catch these hands first!"

"Yo, chill," Bucky said.

"Nah, you fucking chill!" V said.

I didn't know V as well as I knew Jordan and Apollo, but I learned more that night. I knew he was the same age as Ceza. I knew he had a younger sister who was friends with my neighbor. I knew he smoked a lot of weed and that, once upon a time, he went to Franklin. I thought he was cool. Anytime I was around him, he never looked for trouble. That night, however, I learned his loyalty and fearlessness.

Now, Bucky wasn't the biggest guy in the room, but he was pretty street. V didn't care. Once Bucky told him to chill, it was on.

V burst through the front door, launched Uche back into the living room, and speared Bucky into the side of the house. At that point, everyone jumped up. Cocoa's friends slid up the couch in fear while Jordan, Apollo, and I ran to the front door to manage the situation. Cocoa followed. When I made it to the front door, V was on top of Bucky, punching him in the face repeatedly.

"You. Stupid. Mother. Fucker," V said, landing a punch with each word.

After recognizing Bucky was hurt, V grabbed him by the arms, dragged him onto the grass, and kicked him in the side. "Get the fuck outta here, bro! Don't you ever do some stupid shit like this again, in your life!" V shouted.

After the loud scuffle, Ceza stood up from the couch. His legs wobbled like a newborn giraffe as he tried to push himself up, his cup of water spilling on the carpet. Cocoa's tall friend guided him up as he tried to steady himself for the journey to the front of the house.

"I dunno if Ceza's gonna make it to the driveway," Jordan joked.

Jordan was right. Ceza didn't.

About halfway to the door, Ceza stumbled to the floor in drunkenness, completely spilling his cup of water everywhere. I could hear Bucky getting up and V shouting at him from the grass. Moments later, I heard a car start and Bucky was gone.

When V and Uche came back inside, Cocoa and her friends were shaken.

Cocoa's tall dark-skinned friend saw V—shirt ripped, covered in blood—and took him into the kitchen to wash him up.

The shorter fair-skinned friend grabbed Uche, and they went into Uche's bedroom, and I finally grabbed Cocoa, and we went into the bathroom next to the garage.

PART III:

COLLEGE

STEVENS - HOBOKEN, FALL 2006

The weekend before college orientation was tumultuous. I had just competed in the final soccer tournament for my club team, and was preparing to transition from high school soccer to college soccer preseason. I ended my senior year of high school soccer with twenty-six goals, fourteen assists, and first-team all-state honors. I was looking forward to being a top performer in college as well.

Bianca, on the other hand, was nervous. I was going away to college, and she was staying back home to take care of her family. Her father had suffered a stroke and wasn't doing too well, so she decided to take online courses at a community college and stick around to support him. When I first committed to Stevens, Bianca was thrilled that I'd only be forty-five minutes away from home, but as it got closer to moving day, she was fearing the change.

She wasn't the only person who had strong feelings about my transition. Ms. Connie was through the roof with excitement.

"Our boys are growing up so fast," she would say with pride. "Now, Mr. Martin, make sure to always lock your room door when you leave. You never know who's drunk and may stumble into the wrong room."

"Okay, Ms. Connie," I'd agree.

"The good thing about going to college so close to home is that you can always go home and do laundry for free."

"That's right, Ms. Connie."

"Remember, schoolwork first. You are on scholarship, that means you need to keep your grades at a certain level to maintain the same level of financial support."

"Thank you, Ms. Connie."

"Make sure you find a group of kids who are focused on their schoolwork and get close to them. They are going to help you develop the positive habits you will need to be successful there."

"That's a good idea, Ms. Connie."

My mother had her own approach.

"How do you feel, Mart?"

"I feel alright, Mom. I'm looking forward to the season."

"What are you most looking forward to?"

"Meeting my teammates, starting the season, learning more about business, being closer to Manhattan."

"That all sounds so good, Mart. I am really proud of you. You worked hard to get here."

"Thanks, Mom. I'm excited about the next step."

It's true, I was excited about going to Stevens. Stevens Institute of Technology stood at the highest point in Hoboken, New Jersey with unobstructed views of the New York City skyline. When you pull up to the top of the hill and onto campus, the first thing you see is a small castle-like structure that acts as a fence to the campus that boasts a cast-iron sign reading: *Stevens 1870.* Beyond the castle-like structure, you are immediately captivated by and impossible view of New York City. At sunset, the golden-red glow of the sky would bounce off the tall windows of skyscrapers and reflect dancing ripples onto the Hudson River.

On move-in day, it was Kane, Ms. Connie, my mother, and I as a group. As we pulled on to campus, a large sign on the building beyond the gates read, *Davis Hall.*

This is where I'll be living.

As I walked up the stairs of Davis Hall, my heart thumped with excitement. The hallway smelled like bleach or some sort of cleaning solution but I didn't mind it, I just wanted to see my room. The moment I opened my door, my breath was taken away.

"Oh, my goodness, would you look at that view! It's so beautiful!" Ms. Connie said.

Damn.

The entire back wall was a window with a perfect view of the financial district in Manhattan.

After Kane, my mother, and Ms. Connie finished helping me unload my things out of Ms. Connie's van, they thought it best they leave before things got too sentimental. As they exited, I gave my mother and Ms. Connie hugs, and Kane and I did our handshake.

"Be Good, Mart," my mother said.

"I will, Mom."

I fell asleep that night in my new dorm room, overlooking the great borough of Manhattan thinking about life and all of the possibilities that lay before me.

TERRANCE

The next morning, I awoke to the sound of keys jingling on the door. Shortly thereafter, in came a six-foot-one gentleman with a beard.

"What's up, dude? I'm Terrance," he said plainly.

"What's good, bro? Martin, nice to meet you. I guess we're roommates," I said nervously.

"Guess so," Terrance said as he rolled his suitcase a little farther into the room and nearer to the vacant bed along the wall.

A woman stepped into the room behind him. "Hi, I'm Terrance's Aunt Lucy. Wow! What a beautiful view you have!'

"Nice to meet you, Aunt Lucy, and yeah, it's nice."

As much as I wanted to be kind and spend more time with my new roommate and his aunt, I needed time to myself. I was excited about finally being away at college, and wanted to absorb this new atmosphere alone, so I took a walk to the cafeteria. *So, this is where I'll be eating.* I walked to the soccer field. *This is where I'll be bustin' heads.* After about an hour, I walked the long grassy hill to highest peak of campus, Castle Point, which had a full panoramic view overlooking the Manhattan Skyline, Jersey City, and West New York. It was majestic. *That's my city. I'm going to be big there.*

After about an hour, I returned to the dorm room to find Terrance alone with his suitcase spilled open on the bed and Lil Wayne blaring out of his phone.

"You bumping that new Weezy too?" I asked.

"Yeah, bwoy!" Terrance said with excitement. "He from weezy-anna like me. I have to."

"Oh, you're from Louisiana? I knew you were from down South because of the accent, but that's cool," I said, making my way over to my bed by the window.

"Yeah, woadie, I been up in Jersey since Katrina, but I'm from down der, fa sho."

Terrance's voice took on a new excitement, as if he was open to being friends. I was starting to feel like we could get along well.

"You ready for the season?" I asked.

"Yeah, woadie, I'll be cool," he responded.

"Yeah, I think we're the only black kids on the team. Shouldn't be a problem," I said confidently.

"I think so too. We'll be cool."

We'll be cool, huh?. We'll be cool.

PRACTICE

Terrance and I were terrible at waking up on time for practice. I would set my alarm for 6:15, exactly forty-five minutes before practice started. The problem was, I was the king of the snooze button.

"Dang, man," Terrance mumbled as I shook his leg.

It was 6:48, and Terrance and I needed to be on the field, in our gear, ready to play by 7:00.

When Terrance and I arrived at practice two minutes before it started, Coach Donaldson walked up to me. He was a medium-build Irishman with dark black hair, a thick black goatee, and very dark brown eyes. His stare was intense. He intimidated me.

"Martin, why are you and Terrance late?"

"We aren't late, Coach. We were right on-time," I said guiltily.

"If you are early, you are on time. If you are on-time, you're late. If you are late, don't come," he replied.

What type of shit is that? Why is he pressing me? Terrance can speak for himself.

"Got it, Coach, won't happen again," I replied, looking at the ground.

After quick salutations with teammates, we took to the field. Terrance was pulled up to play with the starters, and I was sent to train with the third string.

Where I was, the assistant coach offered us some light directives, mostly running, a few relatively serious drills, but nothing worth anything. *This is bullshit. Whatever, I'm excited to see what my first classes are like.*

When I was in class, I listened and tried my best to pay attention. Every once in a while, I'd either text Bianca or I'd try to catch the eye of a girl in class. Being one of no more than three black kids in any classroom at any given moment, I knew I stood out. I wanted to use that to my advantage. All I needed to do was say or do something that got a cute girl to look at me, and when I looked back, I'd be able to tell if she was attracted to me or not. That's right—I was girl crazy.

One day after class, I went online and noticed that I'd received a message from a girl in Clearwater, Florida.

Damn, she fine. This can't actually be her.

Hey, I love your style, what's up? she messaged.

I like your style too. I'm chillin'. What's good with you? I replied quickly.

Chillin', bored, listening to this Lloyd Banks mixtape, she answered.

I was getting skeptical. *She's too bad, yo.* I decided to ask for her phone number to check and make sure she was real.

It's 813-555-8374. Call me.

So I did. The phone rang, and a young female answered.

"Hey!"

Oh, shit, she's real.

"Crystal?"

"Yeah, what's up? Hehe, you actually called."

After a few tense moments of awkward banter, we found our groove.

We ended up talking on the phone for over an hour, laughing, discussing about our favorite music, favorite clothing brands, comedians, food—you name it. She told me that she was a model and looking to move to New York to pursue modeling and acting. I'd only seen photos and had one conversation with her, and I was interested.

"You should come up to New York," I said.

"I'm thinking of moving up soon, will you spend time with me if I do?"

Oh, shit.

"For sure. Yeah," I said casually as if I hung out with models all the time. *What am I thinking?*

Right at that moment, Bianca called me. *Yeah, okay. Not answering that. I'll call her back later.* I sent Bianca's call to voicemail.

"Great, I can't wait to spend time with you. You're really cool," she said.

I couldn't believe it. *I officially date models.* The girls in class meant little after that.

I called Bianca shortly after getting off the phone with Crystal, but I was only doing it as a motion. The call was short-lived. I told her I was tired from practice and had to train early in the morning, so I had to get to sleep. Once I hung up the phone, I felt a deep sense of relief. *No more obligations for the day.* I put some beats on and started writing a rap verse. After about forty-five minutes of writing, I turned my desk lamp off and went to sleep.

KANE VISITS - HOBOKEN, SPRING 2007

A few friends and I were playing Monopoly in my room when Kane first came to stay with me at college. It was a humid, cloudy day in April. One of those days brightened by the whiteness of the sky, but also dimmed by its grayness. I had just landed on New York Avenue—the final piece I needed to own all the orange properties in Monopoly—when Kane called me to let me know he was downstairs. I ashed the blunt and made my way through the dormitory to get him. When I arrived at the door, Kane had a huge smile on his face.

We had an awesome time that weekend. First, we went and played pick-up soccer with members of the soccer team. Next, we went out to a frat party where Kane hooked up with a girl. The next morning, he showed up at my dorm with blood-shot eyes and a big smile.

"You been smiling all weekend, huh?" I joked.

"Martin, I'm proud of you," Kane said. "Everything you wanted, you went out and got it. You're at an awesome school. You're a part of an incredible college soccer program, and you're rapping. I don't mean to get sentimental, but I want you to know that you are my best friend and I look up to you. I've watched you grow to build a great life for yourself, and I am looking forward to watching you go on to do great things."

"You and that girl must've had a good time last night," I joked.

"No, really. Thank you, Martin, for giving me such a great experience and something to look up to."

Kane had grown at least six inches since the last time I'd seen him. He had grown up. And as proud of me as he may have been, I was much prouder of him.

THE STORY OF TOBI

MANHATTAN, SPRING 2007

Daniel "Tobi" Katobi was an enigma. He was of medium, slender build with caramel skin. He had a small chest with narrow shoulders and a gentle slouch. His face wasn't handsome by conventional standards, but when he smiled his eyes twinkled like minerals in an oceanside stone. On the other hand, when he was sad or concerned, his eyes held a deep longing that carried the pain of conquered nations.

After a failed year of college studying film, he moved from Cleveland, Ohio to New York City. He still loved storytelling but decided he wanted to choose a new medium—music. He believed the greatest human virtue was to inspire. He felt that to take your experience and share its lessons with the world was the greatest gift you could give humanity.

New York was exciting in his first few weeks. He had no trouble making friends at local bars in Manhattan and Brooklyn. He even met a girl, Lisa, from New Jersey who didn't mind that he didn't have a job. In fact, she was in awe that he moved from Cleveland in pursuit of something so elusive. But time had begun to catch up with him, and he was running out of money. Months had gone by and he couldn't find steady work. He was having trouble staying motivated. To numb the pain of uncertainty, he was becoming easily distracted by happy hours, drugs, women, and all the things one could get into in Manhattan. He soon found himself down-and-out, with little prospect for future success.

Tobi was living with his father's brother, Uncle Ahmad, in a one-bedroom apartment in the Bronx. Uncle Ahmad was a small, gentle man with little hands who played the saxophone for a local blues quartet in the South Bronx. He had lived in New York for fifty years working in music full-time, and wanted to support Tobi in his dreams to do the same.

AUDITION

One day, Tobi caught a break. After a chance meeting with a booking agent at a bar in Williamsburg, he was sent to an audition for the role of a football player in a production taking place in the fall. The role paid $500 a day for shooting. *I could use that,* Tobi thought.

The receptionist was a wide-eyed brunette from New Jersey with big teeth, lean lips, and a small hoop earring.

Damn, Mama. Looking good, Tobi thought.

"Daniel Katobi?"

Tobi nodded and was led into a room where the directors wated for him. To Tobi's surprise, the room was dimly lit with spotty, old blue carpeting, and the walls were half wood paneling from floor to midway, half wallpaper from midway to the ceiling, with two small windows along the backside of the room facing a brick wall.

The two directors sat at a fold-out table with four piles of papers, coffee mugs, a few pens, and a timer. One of was them a Middle-Eastern-looking woman, who seemed to be in her mid-forties. *She's prolly like sixty though.* The other was a twenty-something white woman, with a long skirt covering her legs and a short, bohemian crop top. She looked like she could be the receptionist's sister. *Prolly is.*

The lack of energy in the room was palpable. The directors had obviously wanted to get through the day, and neither of them made much of an effort to get to know Tobi.

"Stand on the X," the older woman demanded as Tobi entered the room.

"Have you read the script?" asked the twenty-some-thing woman.

"Yes."

"Excellent. Go," said the twenty-something director, as she waved her hand to send Tobi to the designated spot.

Tobi was a bit startled by how fast this was all moving, but he made his way to the red 'X' and cleared his throat before beginning.

"I don't think we're going to be able to make this work," Tobi started. "As much as I love you, I just can't forgive you for what you've done. You broke my trust." Tobi paused and looked down solemnly. He then put his right hand in his pocket and, with his left hand, motioned for someone to come closer. "I'm going to go, but before I do, I want to give you something...It's a rock from Coney Island that night we fell asleep there. I want you to have it." He paused. "To know that even though I can't be with you, I will always love you." Tobi paused and stared deeply into space.

The twenty-something bohemian director dryly read, "Crying. Crying. Crying…Please, can we try to make this work?"

Tobi responded, "I can't, I'm sorry. Here." Tobi motioned as if handing something to someone, turned, and walked away.

"Scene," said the elder director.

"What y'all think?: Tobi injected.

The twenty-something director leaned forward and smiled, sliding her hands down her thighs.

"Alright, now let's do when Malcolm is hurt at the football game and sees Lucy in the stands," she said in a soft, breathy tone.

Tobi cleared his throat as he made his way to the small blue 'X' on the other side of the room. He took a seat on the ground and pretended to take a sip of a sports drink. He then winced as if struggling through great pain.

"I don't' know, Coach! I heard a pop! Ahhh," he said, grunting while grabbing his left knee.

"Dang, man!" He started to rock back and forth as if the pain was getting stronger. "I really don't know if…" Tobi paused and looked into the distance, as if noticing something familiar but unwelcome. He took a deep gulp.

The elder director's eyes widened.

Tobi held the pause and then said, "I...I'm good, Coach. I can play."

"Are you sure?" asked the twenty-something director.

"Yes, Coach, let me run the next play, I'm good." Tobi fixed his eyes back on the same spot in the distance. "I got this..."

"Scene," said the elder director. "Not bad, thank you. We will be contacting you if you've gotten the part."

"That's all?" Tobi asked.

"Yes. Thank you," said the elder director.

"Bye, Daniel," the twenty-something director said, biting her lip.

"Alright, thank you," Tobi said, turning to leave the room.

When Tobi departed, he found a waiting room full of young black men, all muscular and cleanly shaven. *Lookin' like the Jets waiting to get pre-season physicals.* He then looked to the receptionist who seemed to be typing something into her phone. *Prolly texting shorty inside the room something. Damn, I'm not getting this job.*

Tobi walked out of the office with his head down, hands in his pockets with his thumbs exposed. *I need a cigarette.* He dug into his pocket for some change to buy a loose cigarette at the bodega in midtown. As he stepped on the elevator, he saw a young black gentleman. Their eyes met and they nodded to one another.

Unlike the New York Jets back there, this guy had a full-grown beard, an over-sized blue New York Yankees baseball cap, and a huge pair of headphones blaring music. Tobi tried to see if he recognized the faint sounds coming from the headphones. He couldn't say he did, but he liked it. He waved his hands in the gentleman's face to get his attention.

"What song is that? It sounds dope," Tobi said.

The gentleman looked up at Tobi, startled. "It's mine, I produced it."

"Oh, yeah?" Tobi asked, pleasantly surprised. "What's good, bro? I'm Tobi."

The gentleman looked at him, his eyes softening. "What's up, man? I'm Dez. Nice to meet you."

ALIENS - MANHATTAN, SUMMER 2007

I met Andy by chance. He was the cousin of a good friend of mine growing up that I met at a barbecue, but we kept in touch. He was Puerto Rican, with long wavy hair, and incredibly generous. One thing I learned quickly about Andy, was his interest in fashion and music. His taste in clothing, style, and art was sharp. When he thought something was hot, it was. He had an eye for aesthetics and an ear for authenticity.

I was lying in bed one night in my dorm room when Andy gave me a call. He told me that he stumbled across a group of young creatives in New York called the A.L.I.E.N crew.

"Bro, these dudes are wearing turban scarves with Nike Cortez's and shirts they designed themselves with African necklaces and skinny jeans and shit. Crazy," Andy said.

They wore vibrant textiles and danced like Michael Jackson on subway trains for fun. They were the type to donate clothes to churches and then scale the fire escapes to smoke weed on the roof. They would spray paint graffiti hearts on the sides of garbage trucks and hand out thesauruses to the homeless. They were free. Social vagabonds crafting an existence authentic to themselves and their city, as proud outcasts. The clothing they wore was so obviously inspired by hip-hop but without its misogynistic undertones or homophobic stigmas. They were accepting, and they were fresh.

"These dudes are it," Andy said. "We gotta get to New York."

And so I went.

It was a beautiful night in August when Andy and I arrived in New York on the day of the *L.A.C.E.D Magazine* release party. Everyone from New York who was interested in footwear, streetwear, and the new creative movement that was brewing was going to be there. The Who's Who of New York City's new school nightlife. Steven "Steve-O" Black, Saint Lewis, Kehmani Kalm, Trickey Stackz, Precsize, Shannon Lambo, Shavonne, LaMont LeCarmen. All of these names that Andy had been following and admiring for months now were at this party.

Andy and I showed up a few minutes past 11 p.m. and made our way to the bar. "That's Trickey Stackz. He raps, but you're nicer than him. That's Steve-O. He manages Trickey and is also a main contributor to the magazine. That's Saint Lewis. He is one of the founders of the magazine and manages Trickey with Steve-O. They both have crazy sneaker collections. They the ones runnin' this shit. That's Shannon Lambo. She fucks with the brand Dauley and Llama as a marketing chick or some shit. And that's LaMont LeCarmen. He runs with the A.L.I.E.N Crew. I found out about the party on his page. Matter o' fact, let's go see if we can talk to him," Andy said with excitement.

As Andy and I tried to get closer to Carmen without him noticing, Carmen spotted Andy's retro cement Jordan 4's and stopped him. "Yo! Bro, those are stupid!"

The two began to connect over the sneakers, and Carmen got really excited. He and Andy ended up talking for thirty minutes right there. I was just sipping water and happy to be in New York at such a cool event.

"Yo, y'all should meet Trickey. He's huge on Jordans," Carmen said.

"Bet!" Andy exclaimed.

Trickey Stackz was a local rapper from the Bronx making a decent name for himself on the underground scene. Carmen walked us over to Trickey, who was surrounded by women near the bar.

"Yo, Trickey. This is Marty and Andy. Andy is a fashion designer and Marty…Wait, Marty, what do you do?"

"I rap."

"Oh, yeah? Let me hear something."

I was prepared for this. I had verses on top of verses written from back in my mom's house for moments like these. I pulled out my favorite one.

"Young troublemaker, turn your girl into a puddle maker
Boy I'm stone-cold undertaker
She was probably under the impression I was gonna date her
But I just let her go ahead like a running pacer
It ain't a problem to me, I'm popping, ya see
Only nineteen with a flow that's unstoppable, G.
Find me on top of a V, that's a W
Untouchable, don't let my bars trouble you
'less I don't fuck with you
Still a youngin', turning twenty in a month or two
You look so uncomfortable, How this even fun for you?"

I'll never forget the way Carmen's eyes lit up. "What!" he shouted. "Ayo, come here. We need to talk."

And just like that, we were in.

OUT - THE BRONX, SUMMER 2007

A few weeks had passed since Tobi left the audition for the daytime TV show playing Malcolm, the football player, and he hadn't gotten a callback. He'd been able to pick up a few extra shifts at American Apparel, but his checks weren't enough to pay for all his travel, food, and still have enough to help his uncle. One night, Tobi walked into his uncle's bedroom to ask him what he wanted for dinner. His uncle had another conversation in mind.

"I can't go another month without some help from you, Daniel," Uncle Ahmad said abruptly.

Tobi was startled. "I'm trying, it's just hard to get a grip, Unc."

His uncle sighed. "It's tough on me, man."

"I know, Unc, but I'm tryna figure it out. You see me busting my ass, don't you?"

"I seen you leave for that audition. Honestly, I ain't seen much since."

"I've been writing, Unc, and I have some really good stuff. I also started working with this producer and we vibe, man. It's special. I don't have much now but I promise you Unc, in a few months, a year tops, we won't have to worry about anything."

Uncle Ahmad looked in Tobi's eyes, as if he remembered that drive, that ambition, that youthful ignorance in himself.

Uncle Ahmad took a seat. He then rubbed the tips of his fingers against his scalp as he set his gaze low, his eyes fixed on a picture on the bottom level of a bookcase across the room. The picture was a photograph of him and five of his old bandmates in 1974 after a performance at the New York Academy of Music. Of all the members of the band in the photo, Uncle Ahmad was the only one to not go on to tour the world and gain international recognition for his work. He had instead chosen to stay in New York and work at The Bronx Conservatory of Jazz Music as Director of Music, where he'd been for the last twenty-five years. He looked away from the photo and back at Tobi as if returning to a reality he had forgotten.

He sat up straight. "Listen, I believe in you, Daniel. I promise I do, but I can't keep this up or we will both be out on the streets, man. Unfortunately." He then softened his shoulders, slouched back down in his seat, and looked back at the photo.

Tobi saw how hard it was for his uncle to have to say this to him. It moved him.

"You know what, Unc?" Tobi said. "You're right. I can't keep doing this to you. I'll go. I've got to figure this out on my own."

Uncle Ahmad raised his eyebrows and slowly extended his little hand to Tobi. "What? You don't have to leave today. I just need you to help take care of the bare necessities. Your own food, electricity from all that time you spend on the computer, help with the water bill from all your showers. Stuff like that."

"I just can't help you with those things right now, Unc. I'm diving into this project, and I'm having trouble finding work. I don't want to be a burden. I'll leave, Unc. I'll come by and visit, but I can't do this to you. It'll kill you." Tobi knelt to be eye level with his Uncle. "I'm not giving up, Unc. No matter what, I'm not giving up. I came to New York for a reason, and I'm going to do it."

Uncle Ahmad was speechless. At the same time, he respected Tobi for it. Tobi was willing to dive into a deeper unknown for his music. Something Uncle Ahmad was unable to do in his youth. "Alright, Daniel. Do as you wish."

Tobi left his Uncle's bedroom and walked to the old desktop computer in the living room to find somewhere to go. At the top of his inbox was a note from Dez.

This is the one, the note stated. *attached.*

Tobi took a deep breath, clicked the file, and began to hum. As he hummed, he responded to the email with a message of his own. *Yo, Dez, I'm gonna need a place to stay while we record this album. You got me?*

He turned and stared out the window as he waited for Dez to respond to his email. *What am I thinking, Dez is gonna think I'm crazy. We've only been working together for a few months and now I'm asking to move in.*

Two minutes later, Tobi got an email response from Dez. *Yeah, bro. I'll make you a key.*

"Damn," Tobi whispered.

And just like that, Tobi was out.

TOBI MOVES IN WITH DEZ, BROOKLYN, SUMMER 2007

Desmond "Dez" Okon was a tall Nigerian introvert. He had the build of a college basketball player, with long muscular arms and a lanky frame. His face was sharp with straight lines and hardened by long winters in New York. He had a dense, well-groomed beard and a wide round nose that supported a pair of spectacles he always pushed up.

Dez grew up in a strict, traditional Nigerian home in Brooklyn. His parents moved to New York in 1972 after the Nigerian Civil war and wanted their children to grow up well-mannered, disciplined, and obedient. Throughout his childhood, Dez was taught to always tuck in his collared shirts, wear bow ties to school, and to never raise his voice. On his tenth birthday, his sister gave him the CD of an artist called Mista Bumpkin. It changed his life forever.

Mista Bumpkin was an eccentric and electric singer, dancer, and performer whose staple was to yell, shout, and scream his lyrics at the top of his lungs. As a child, Dez would play Mista Bumpkin through headphones and lip-sync the screams emphatically. Since he wasn't allowed to raise his voice, this was a therapeutic exercise for him. He found that music was an opportunity to express himself vicariously through someone else. That feeling fueled his love for music and his eventual desire to bring that feeling forward to others.

On Tobi's first night at Dez's parents' house, he couldn't sleep. He found himself staring at the ceiling from the mattress on the floor in Dez's sister's old bedroom. Everything was loud. The cracks of the wood on the ground, the exposed brick on the wall, the sounds of subways in the distance. Dust particles floated through a faint beam of light showing through the window of an adjacent apartment, bouncing off his eyes as he gazed solemnly into the darkness. He couldn't sleep. He wasn't sure if he wanted to sleep, but he knew he didn't want to be awake.

On the floor next to the mattress was a mug that read *Happy Mother's Day* half-filled with over-steeped peppermint tea that he'd poured but had forgotten to drink.

Basking in the depths of his emotions, he sat up, leaned his back against the exposed brick wall, and looked around the room. The reality of the moment scared him. He wasn't in Cleveland. He wasn't at Uncle Ahmad's. He was somewhere else. He was in someone's family home in Brooklyn on a mattress on the floor. *Why me? I ain't shit, man. Here I am, in this room, on this fuckin' floor. I'm worthless. I'm a con artist. What am I even trying to do? Who do I think I am?* He sighed deeply.

He began to twirl pieces of his hair together as he peered into the blurry dimness of the room. His eyes adjusted a bit more, and he was able to see the plastic bag filled with his clothes across the room. *Dez and I are gonna finish this project, and it's gonna all come together. I don't need nobody to believe in me.* His thoughts were getting louder. *You don't got it, bro! You're fucking broke, fool!* His heart began to beat faster as his back slid down the wall. He then rolled to one side and crossed his hands under his head. *Stop it!*

He couldn't control this internal dialogue. His fears and worries consumed him. He lay there the rest of the night, battling with the demon of despair.

The next afternoon, Tobi walked into Dez's bedroom, still tired from lack of sleep. "Go back to what we started working on yesterday. That gentle shit." Tobi took a pull of the blunt as he put his headphones on.

"Put the lows on the outsides…No. No. No…The four lows there…Yeah, and then highs on top, panned out…Lemme hear that."

Dez played back the record.

"Lower the volume on the panned highs and raise the volume on the lowest lows, let me hear that."

Dez made the adjustments.

"Cool…Now I'ma go in and fill in the middle with that shit I was humming out earlier."

"I fuck with that," Dez said.

Tobi tapped the tip of the blunt on the edge of the Sprite can, making his way to his headphones at rest on Dez's bed.

Dez's bedroom was no different than any other Brooklyn bedroom: black bars lined thin, cloudy windows, a dresser that his grandmother passed down to his mother covered in Japanese magazines, Dutchmaster blunt wraps, coins, a hair comb, old mail, some open and some unopened, and empty soda cans for ashing out cigarettes and blunts.

Tobi began to hum into the mic, testing the volume of the microphone's voice reception but also the timbre in his voice. *Do I like my voice right now?*

"Aight, run it," he said.

Tobi closed his eyes.

As the soft guitar sample played in Tobi's ears, he was transported. He was no longer in Dez's room. He was in a world within his own mind. He was in his house of mirrors. Staring at himself within his own mind, he had a message. He began to sing.

"Why do you look at me, So?
Are you afraid? I don't know
Maybe I should stay alone
Would you be better off?
Could I be better?

Why don't I see through your lies?
No matter how many tries
You are so good at disguise
Could you just take it off?
Or should I just take it?

These thoughts run through my head
As I lay in this bed
These internal fights
On these sleepless nights"

"Aight, cut it."

Dez stopped the recording.

"Aight...What you think?" Tobi asked

"Perfect. How'd that feel?"

"Nigga! Like therapy!"

They both laughed.

"Perfect," Dez responded. "Absolutely perfect."

SWAY - TRIBECA, WINTER 2007/2008

LaMont LeCarmen was the most charismatic person I had
ever met. He was full of life, energy, and hope for the future.
It was if he always knew he was going to arrive, he just didn't
know when. He stood at about five-foot-six, slender with long,
soft muscles. He walked swiftly, with a slight slouch, and took
small, graceful steps. He had a warm, inviting face, with a
short, round nose, a large mouth, long and narrow, with big
teeth that gave him the appearance of an eternal smile. His
skin—a rich dark brown that lightened in his face—offered
him a luminescence regardless of the lighting. He spoke with

a raspy, throaty voice that communicated the same fluency as his movements.

His mind was sharp and courageous in its ambition. He held an acute understanding of motive and intention, and was able to brilliantly manage both when dealing with others. One night, he invited me to a lounge in Tribeca called Sway that had a crazy Monday night party called *Electric Punnany*.

"There is nowhere on earth like Sway lounge," he told me.

He was right. Sway was a drug. It was the epicenter of forbidden youth. A fountain of debauchery and degenerate chic. On any given night, you could find the new young movie star, the local celebrity, the drug dealer, the college girls from Sweden in on vacation, the iconic rockstar, and the rising young comedian all in the bar at the same time.

Out front of Sway were two big bouncers, James and Barkley. James was the head of security, a big burly bear of a man who meant straight business. Barkley was burly as well, but much younger than James. James sat on a stool and Barkley stood next to the stool. Anyone who has any club bouncer friends knows that they are big babies. Barkley was no exception. In fact, neither were exceptions. They were both big lovable babies.

I was a bit nervous because I was only nineteen—two years below the minimum age to get in the lounge—but Carmen ensured me that I didn't have to worry.

From down the street, Barkley yelled, "Who's this stinky thirsty Staten Island nigga coming down the block?"

Carmen returned, "What do we have here? I think two sloppy ass meatballs rolled off someone's plate and landed in front of Sway!"

"Keep talking that slick shit and these balls gon' meet your face!"

That was a good one.

"That's gross! You're gonna make me throw up. Your balls probably look like shriveled up dates in an old vacuum-sealed bag!"

"Why don't you come get a closer look, you dusty ass subway rat!"

"What did I tell you about putting rats in your pants, bro? They don't belong there, cut it out!"

They both laughed and then embraced, Barkley bear hugging Carmen and shaking him. "You know I love you. What's up with you, Big B, how are you?" Carmen asked as Barkley gently lowered him down.

"I'm good, man…can't complain. I mean I can, but I won't, unless one of these motherfuckers start acting stupid."

"Haha, I hear that. Aye, B, this is my boy Marty. Next big thing in hip-hop, I'm telling you."

Barkley looked at me. "Is that right? Spit something right now."

I knew it was a test. What he was really asking me was, "Do you believe in yourself?" I knew that all I had to do was have that one line that showed him how my mind worked. That one line that proved I had a special ability, the agility to manipulate words through space and time unscripted. *Just one needs to cut deep. Go!*

"In the front of Sway like, Aye! No, I don't play
Since I'm a pro-teen; they tryna get in my whey
Incredibly fresh face, look like I was born today
My skin is what gets me in; my talent's what makes me stay."

"Oh, shit," said Barkley.

"Big B is the big homie, who barely know me
Carmen told 'em I could spit, so he looked at me like 'Show me'
Ha! I assume the challenge and resume my talents
They think being black and intelligent is an
unusual balance."

"Whoa!" Barkley exclaimed. He was nodding his head and rubbing his hands together. He was starting to feel it. I was starting to feel it. We were almost there. Nirvana. I could feel other people beginning to close in around us in admiration.

"Well, here it is! Impeccably spirited
Respected and feared, as special as erecting the pyramids!"

"Oh!" the group roared.

I could feel Carmen's arm on my shoulder, protecting me, encouraging me. I needed him. He let out a loud "Ah!" after every line I spoke, as if he had just taken a huge swig of soda with a large smile on his face as he looked around at the growing crowd. By now, camera lights were in our faces. *Don't be nervous. Keep going. Carmen's got you.*

"Are you F'in serious?
I am at the intersection of curious, and furious
Lesson? Never question me, period!"

The front of Sway exploded in excitement and admiration fell upon my shoulders. Carmen quickly yanked me away, pulling me inside before anyone could touch me.

THE LABEL - MANHATTAN, SPRING 2008

Tobi and Dez got off the subway at 34th and Broadway and made the first left on to 35th Street. They walked past the bodega that sold loose cigarettes, the Turkish restaurant, Chobana, with the blue awning that needed to be repainted, and past the new coffee shop, Sips, until they reached the Gartner Music Building, a towering structure, the ninth highest building in New York City.

"Executive Suite 1706…Does that mean the seventeenth floor?" Dez asked, confused.

"Man, I don't know. Let's ask the receptionist when we get in there," Tobi replied.

Tobi was beginning to get anxious, so he turned around, walked two blocks back to the bodega, and bought a few loose cigarettes. He always smoked when he got anxious.

After some calming pulls of the cigarette, Tobi's nervousness turned into anticipation and confidence.

"We finna go up in this building and walk out with a record deal, bro. The world needs this music. Ain't no one making real shit like this. If these motherfuckers don't fuck with this music, then we move on to someone who will. It's that simple."

"Bro, you already know," Dez confirmed.

Tobi and Dez made their way to the elevator. It was happening. Tobi was getting closer to his dream. His hands were trembling with excitement as he visualized Simple Sam handing him a contract, changing his life. Tobi knew he and Dez had created a masterpiece, and no one could tell him any different.

Dez looked at Tobi and smiled as they walked through the hallways of the large building.

There were three people in the meeting room when they arrived. Closest to the door, and the first to greet them, was Samuel "Simple Sam" Jones, a music A&R responsible for big acts like Tunji, Pony People, Nothing Special, Dig Bifference, and G.I.R.L.

"What's good, y'all? I'm Tobi."

"And I'm Dez."

"Tobi…Dez…Nice to meet you both, I'd like you to meet Patrick McGivalry, SVP of Urban Entertainment, and Scram Jackson, Touring Director for Sound Gravity."

"Nice to meet you both," said Tobi, leaning in with excitement.

"Absolutely. Absolutely. Simple Sam has said great things about you. Have a seat!" McGivalry said, adjusting his already perfectly tied tie.

Patrick McGivalry was a no-nonsense man. He had a strong towering build, bushy unwavering eyebrows, and a very deep voice. He rarely smiled, but when he did, he was like a child. He always went to work in a blue suit and black tie. He'd been at the label for eight years and hadn't worn anything other than a blue suit, black tie, and shiny black shoes—even when he was an intern.

All five men sat down. Tobi was confident in his music, but unsure how the gentlemen would respond to it. He went around playing music for people all the time, but something was different about this meeting. He had expectations. He wanted them to *like* what he made. He knew that if they liked it and gave him a shot, his music would reach the masses. That was all that mattered to him. That his music reached as many people as possible. This was his greatest opportunity yet.

I wonder if they gonna like my shit.

"So, it is obvious that you are making quite a buzz around the city with 'Sleepless Nights,' a little over twenty-five thousand streams in your first week, and as of this morning, you are at five hundred thousand total streams. That's pretty good, people are listening," McGivalry said.

Tobi laughed nervously. "Last time I checked, it was at fifteen thousand, so that's cool," he said, trying to hide a prideful smile. Dez sat quietly, obediently. "You know, Dez and I recorded that and the majority of our project in his bedroom and I'm telling y'all, it's all magic. Dez is a beast, yo. But... you know, I came here to play my music for you and see what y'all think and see what we can do together, and like, I like talking to y'all and I want to meet and stuff, but is it cool if we talk after y'all hear the music?"

Simple Sam smiled.

"Sure," said, McGivalry. "Do you have the music on CD or your phone?"

"I have a CD, fa sho," Tobi replied, opening his jacket and removing the disc.

Simple Sam then leaned over and pushed down on a small square cut-out in the middle of the table. The small cut-out slowly flipped over and a flat circle appeared within the square's underside, to put a CD on.

These niggas.

"Put the CD on there, and it will play on the speakers in all corners of the room," Simple Sam explained.

"Cool, thanks," Tobi replied, awkwardly placing the disc on the flat circle.

Tobi placed the disc on the circle in the middle of the table. Once the disc was secure, the square then flipped again and receded back into the table.

"I'ma get that back, right?" Tobi joked.

"Not if it's good," Simple Sam responded.

Intro music played.

"The motivation for my new album is bringing authenticity back to the forefront, bringing real content, bringing real emotion, the realness. And I'm not talking about street realness. Fuck your money. Fuck your jewelry. Fuck your cars. Fuck all bitches that you get—that just don't make you cool. You are obsolete now."

The beat dropped, and the first song began.

At the end of the intro, no one said anything. The second song played. Silence. Then the third song played. Still nothing. Tobi opened his eyes, seeing that everyone but Dez had their eyes closed. When the beat dropped for the beginning of the fourth song, Scram began to nod his head.

He fucks with this one.

Tobi peeked over at Dez and saw him smilingly proudly.

All eight tracks played through. Twenty-nine minutes and forty-four seconds in total, and no one had said a word.

McGivalry was the first one to speak. "So, what'd you guys come here for?"

"I came for you to listen to my music and to see if it makes sense for us to work together," Tobi replied, sitting up straight in his chair. He noticed a glimmer in McGivalry's eyes.

He liked it.

"What is it that you want?" McGivalry clarified.

"I want my music to reach as many people as possible. I want for the kids who feel misunderstood to know that it is okay. For them to know that there is someone out there like them, who understands them and who isn't judging them for being themselves. You know, coming up, everyone is so judgmental. You have to be this, you have to be that. At some point, I said, 'No, I'm going to do what I want. Life is about doing what makes you happy, you know.' and so I want the little homies out there to hear that message coming from the music. And that's my music." Tobi said, passionately.

McGivalry stared at Tobi. Simple Sam smiled.

"And what do you want?" McGivalry asked, turning to Dez.

"To make the biggest songs in the world," Dez replied.

McGivalry adjusted his seat and said dryly, "Your numbers are decent, but not incredible. I think with a little polishing, you can be alright."

Tobi rolled his eyes.

McGivalry continued, "How about this, when you get your plays to a million, come back. You'll be ready then. Your stuff is good but after one million, come back."

Tobi looked at Simple Sam. Simple Sam looked away in frustration. Tobi looked at Scram. Nothing.

Tobi looked quickly at Dez and then back at McGivalry. "Thank you for listening to our music. Y'all take care now."

Never Again, Tobi thought. *Never Again.*

QUIT - HOBOKEN, SPRING 2008

I'd spent the last year in and out of studios with Carmen. He completely took me under his wing. He introduced me to everyone he knew as the next big thing in hip-hop, and he knew a lot of people.

"Yo, this is Marty, remember this face," or "Yo, Marty, spit something light. Just a little, you know," or "Wait until you hear Marty's tracks yo, crazy!"

Every night of the week, Carmen and I would either be at fancy lounges in and around New York running around with girls, visual artists, fashion designers, professional skate-boarders, and musicians, or we would be in some studio somewhere in Manhattan working on music until the wee hours of the morning. It was exhilarating. The problem was, I was exhausted. I'd come home from Manhattan at 3 a.m. and have to wake up for soccer practice at 6:15, followed by a full day of classes. It was brutal. I had to make a decision.

On a warm spring day, I walked into Coach Donaldson's office to let him know I appreciated the opportunity he provided me in recruiting me for the soccer program at Stevens, but I had to pursue what was most important to me—music. Soccer got me into Stevens; music was going to get me out.

"Martin, are you sure this is something you want to do? We value you so much," Coach said. His dark eyes fixed on me. I wanted to look away, but I had to stand up to him.

"Thanks, Coach, but I'm sure. I want to make music," I replied.

His office was cold, but bright. It was an uncomfortable balance.

"Your teammates will miss your presence," he said calmly.

"I know, Coach, I had a great time with them, but I'll still be on campus," I replied, maintaining eye contact.

"After some more work, I was planning to make you a starter." He placed one hand on his desk and the other on his chin.

"That is kind of you, Coach, but I have to go."

I knew what he was trying to do, and I wasn't going to let him. This was my time. I was tired of driving his narrative forward, being a pawn in his game so he could win a championship. I had to be firm. Otherwise, I'd never be able to trust myself to make a challenging decision ever again.

Quitting the soccer team meant for the first time in almost ten years, I wouldn't be playing competitive soccer. Every weekend for the last decade, I'd had a game. This wasn't just a change in schedule; this was a total change in lifestyle. It was a big decision, and one I knew I had to make.

"Will you still be in school?"

"Yes."

"Is your mother aware of your decision?" he asked, tilting his head.

Mom. He's right. I had not considered anyone else in my decision. For a moment, I hesitated. I questioned whether I was being too impulsive. I could feel the warmth of his stare on my face. *He's winning.* I had to get it together, regain my composure, and be decisive. I shifted in my seat and looked deeper into his eyes. For the first time, I could see where the black of his pupil met the deep dark brown of his iris.

"She understands me," I said.

He broke my stare and looked out the window. He let out a deep sigh, took his hand off his desk.

He's giving up. I won.

"Well," he started. "Let me know if you want to come back to the team. You are always welcome, Martin."

"Okay. Thank you."

I left his office with my chin held high. As I walked back to my dorm, I couldn't help but think, *I'm free.* I was no longer beholden to another man's schedule. I no longer had to fight for the approval of someone I feared. I now had the time to learn who I really was and develop myself into who I wanted to be.

SIMPLE SAM - THE LOWER EAST SIDE, SUMMER 2008

Tobi walked into Fat Baby's Tavern in the Lower East Side of Manhattan, walked up to the bar, and ordered a Pabst Blue Ribbon. It was your typical night at Fat Baby's, hipsters shaking about—young guys and girls on the dance floor—when Tobi noticed a familiar face by the bar. It was Simple Sam, from the record label. Tobi walked right up to him.

"Ay, Sam, what's good?" Tobi asked aggressively.

"Wow, Tobi, crazy seeing you. Man, I've been listening to your mixtape in my car ever since you came up to the label, dude. It's incredible."

Tobi's guard fell. He could sense the sincerity in Simple Sam's voice. "Yeah? That's cool, man. Thank you."

"Seriously, it's really good."

"I appreciate that. That's dope…"

"What you been up to?"

"I been aight, man. Working with Dez on getting more songs together. Grinding, bro, non-stop. What about you?"

"I'm good. I left the label, man."

"Did you?"

"Yeah, I felt like it was time for a change. I've been feeling it for a while."

Tobi paused. He took a good look at Sam.

"You won't get it back if it's good," Tobi remembered.

"You want to manage me?" Tobi asked abruptly.

"I thought you'd never ask."

THE STORY OF APOLLO

———

APOLLO, SUMMER 2009

After graduating college, Apollo had a rough time finding work. He was unsure what he wanted to do, who he wanted to be, and what he wanted to have. He had spent so much of his life being known as "the kid who had his stuff together" that he struggled when it seemed as though that was no longer reality. He tried to stick it out in Atlanta after graduation, but after a few months the money dried up. He decided to move back home to Franklin for a few months to regroup.

At first, it was fine. Apollo would send out applications to marketing agencies in New York during the day and spend time with old friends at night. However, when a few months went by with no job prospects in sight, his parents began to apply some pressure.

"Apollo, you need to get a job," his father would say.

"You aren't looking hard enough," his mother would argue.

After a few months of this, Apollo relented and found a job in Erie, Pennsylvania as a Marketing Manager for a national light bulb manufacturer. The position paid $50,000 a year, which was more money than he had ever made. Though reluctant, he accepted the position and moved to Erie at the end of September for a crisp October 1st start date.

THE PARKING LOT – JERSEY CITY, FALL 2009

Jordan: *Yo, I'm outside.*

Me: *Cool, I'll be down in a sec.*

That night, Jordan picked me up from Stevens to freestyle battle the best rapper on his campus, this kid they called Fresh, a Jersey City local and well known in town for being an incredible freestyler. I'd heard stories about him embarrassing a guy in front of his girlfriend, and the girl driving off with Fresh that same night. Jordan kept me calm though. He wasted no time in letting me know how excited he was.

"Bro, he literally has nothing for you. I can't wait to see this shit. You are going to annihilate his ass."

When we arrived on Jordan's campus, there was an electric energy in the air. Rumors had started to spread around campus that someone had arrived to battle Fresh. As I walked from the MDX to the parking lot where the battle would go down, I could hear a distant mumble. *Sounds like a lot of people.* As we drew closer, people walked up to us excitedly.

"You the one battling Fresh?" one cute Spanish girl asked me.

"Yeah," I responded with soft eyes.

She looked me up and down in admiration. "Okay, I'll see you after," she said and walked off.

Jordan smiled. "Man, this is gonna be great," he said, rubbing the palms of his hands together.

We turned the corner into the second parking lot and it was an absolute zoo. There must have been at least two hundred people waiting for this battle. *Oh, shit. You better get his ass.*

I think Jordan could sense the change in my heart rate. He leaned over to me and said, "Fuck them, eat him." That was all I needed. I was taken back to half-time against North Hunterdon. Jordan was with me and believed in me. I jumped on top of the car, shook Fresh's hand, and got right to it.

"They should pull out cameras and make a documentary
'Bout how I came in this bitch and made your block remember me!
I'm casual, you see what I'm on, I'm barely trying
You're a fraud! Pretending your whole life like, 'I'm barely lying!'
With your all-black shades on, the smartest thing you did
In anticipation of my arrival, cause I'm shinin' on the kid
'Bout to take your girl to a party, have her grindin' on the kid
She pushing back with so much pressure, could make a
diamond on the kid!
But look, they brought the king to a rook, we're playing chess
Now you shook, your biggest mistake was saying yes
I'm sorry I had to end your career so quickly
You look like Bobby Brown, but you act so Whitney
I thought you were in sync, but you talk so Britney."

I turned to the crowd.

"I got him peeing on himself like he got no kidneys!"

The entire parking lot erupted. Some people rocking cars, others were honking horns. It was madness. When I got down from the car we were standing on, I felt someone tugging on my shirt. It was the cute Spanish girl from earlier.

I looked at Jordan. "Let me get the keys."

She and I walked off holding hands on our way to the MDX.

NEVER STOP - JERSEY CITY, WINTER 2009

Jordan and I hopped out of the MDX having stopped at Checkers on the way to Jersey City from Hoboken. We had some weed, some DutchMasters, Checkers chili cheese fries, T-Mobile sidekicks, and a car. What else did we need? Two young, handsome, black boys with the world ahead of them. To us, we had already made it. We were in college, doing what we loved and hooking up with the girls we were attracted to. We were alive.

On that night, Jordan and I were on our way to meet up with his friend Lisa who had a boyfriend that made music and was beginning to gain popularity. I had already beaten Fresh, so I felt invincible when I stepped on that campus. "Tell him to bring his A-game," I said boastfully.

When Jordan and I arrived on campus, it was particularly quiet for a Friday night. No one was in the parking lot. No one was in the lobby. No one was in the hallways. When Jordan and I approached Lisa's dorm room, the door was already open, music was playing, and a gentleman leaned out a window smoking a blunt.

Oh, shit. That guy looks cool.

"Yo?" Jordan said as he gently opened the door to the suite.

The gentlemen turned and looked at us as we entered the room.

"Ay, Jordan, what's good, bro?" the gentleman said with excitement.

"Tobi, what's up, bro!" Jordan said, matching the gentleman's energy as he leaned in to embrace.

Jordan knows him?

A young woman entered the room gingerly, as if to respect our discussion. She had pale white skin, long brown hair to her shoulders, and a navy blue romper that flowed from side to side. *She looks rich. Must be Lisa.*

"Ay! Lisa, what's good, homie!" Jordan asked.

"Hey, Jordan, how you doing?" she said as she leaned in and air-kissed the sides of his face, one cheek after the other.

"Ain't shit, this is my little brother, Marty, I was telling you about," Jordan replied. He never waited to introduce me, and I was very proud and appreciative of that.

I wonder if she'll like me.

"Marty, it's so nice to meet you! I've heard your music and I love it!"

She likes me. "Thank you," I said.

"I see you've met my boyfriend, Tobi. Tobi, this is the Marty I was telling you about."

"What's good, bro?" Tobi said with a smile, leaning in to dap me up. As I got closer, I felt an uneasy tremble in my throat. My hands began to sweat and my body stiffened.

"I'm good," I said casually, trying to mask what I was feeling inside. "Chillin', just got this Checkers, finna roll-up." I was rambling. I didn't know to say. I felt the need to fill any and all silence in the room. My thoughts were so loud, I feared that if no one was speaking, everyone would hear them.

"Yeah, you can always catch me posted with a blunt and a brew, my dude. I'll roll something up too. I'm gonna smoke this one to the face and then come fuck wit' y'all," Tobi said definitively. "I'ma be in there in a sec, just gotta shake these fucking jitters, feel me."

"Word," Jordan responded.

Jitters? Is he nervous to meet me?

Lisa led Jordan and me into the living room. It room was modest with two small wooden chairs, a love seat, and a square, pine table. Jordan and I pulled the two chairs out from under the small table. I peered behind Jordan's head to have a look into the kitchen. *That fit is fire.*

"So, Lisa! What's good!" Jordan shouted.

"Ain't shit, Jordan. Tobi and I are just chilling. We were waiting on you guys," Lisa responded. "Marty, it's so nice to meet you, Jordan played me your stuff and it's dope."

"Thank you."

"I think you and Tobi are really gonna vibe for sure."

"Cool, thank you. Yeah, I'm about to roll something up right now."

A few minutes later, Tobi came into the room. He took a seat next to Lisa on the small couch and used the edge of the table to crack open a beer. I had just finished rolling up a new blunt and decided to light it. Tobi shuffled in his seat. Lisa leaned forward, slid her hands down her legs, and rested them in a fist between her thighs. Jordan smiled. He then dug into his pocket for his phone and grabbed the auxiliary cord that connected to the two external speakers on the table.

"I know y'all got bars for this…" Jordan said with a sly smile on his face, as he plugged in and played an instrumental.

I closed my eyes. *Breathe.*

I let Tobi's instrumental move me. *What is this beat trying to tell me? Ah, I got it.*

"*Picture me, picture me, picture me making history*
Sidestepping the fakes, high-stepping the snakes
Walking through tall grass while fall passes
Designer fashions, scarfs you couldn't imagine
Player'd up, layered up, flavored Dutch
Mayor'd up with a bad bitch in her favorite stuff
….and I'm playing Madison Square
Look at what's happening here
Blunt smoking and sipping
Once the trunk opens, they dippin'
Send something straight at your Pippen's
I tell em…picture me…picture me…
Paint a vivid picture how I'm living."

"Aye!" Jordan exclaimed.

"Wow," Lisa said softly.

Tobi nodded pensively, yet approvingly. The beat continued and Tobi followed up.

::Humming::
"*Roll up…something crazy*

Smoke to keep the bad thoughts away
I tell my demons, no not today
Uh-Uh
Mama wanted me to go to college
Uh-Uh

Now Mama see what's in my wallet
Uh-Huh
Fuck a cap-n-gown, I be cappin' clowns
I don't need to walk across a stage—I'd rather rage
Graduated to be the most celebrated
The weed keeps me elevated
The liquor keeps me feeling nice while I provide...
The funky shit that'll hit your mind like a Tsunami
While these other dudes fold, like origami."

I had goosebumps. There was something about the way Tobi expressed himself that touched me. When he said, "I tell my demons, no, not today," it felt *real*. It didn't feel like he was rapping. It felt like he was telling me something in confidence. Like he was telling me a secret I couldn't tell anyone. I felt closer to him.

Almost immediately after he said "origami," he moved on.

"Bro, is it cool if I play you some songs off my project?" he asked.

"Yeah, please," I responded quickly.

Jordan removed his phone from the auxiliary cord and plugged in Tobi's. We started from the first song on his project.

After the first song finished, I thought, *Wow, this reminds me of Tunji.*

All eight tracks played through and no one had said a word.

Tobi was the first to speak up. "What y'all think?"

"That was dope, man. Thank you for sharing," I said.

"Thank y'all for listening. Is it cool if I step out and have a cigarette?" Tobi said.

I found it odd that he wanted to step out so quickly, but I couldn't not let him have a cigarette. So I offered to join him.

"Yeah, I'll come wit' you?" I said, trying to sound a bit cooler than I felt at the time.

"Fa sho. Let's go."

When Tobi and I left the dorm room, the hallways and the lobby were still empty, as if Tobi and I were the only two people left on the planet.

"Something I realize about a lot of ambitious people is that they get caught up in what they aren't yet to the point where it stops them from growing," he said. "The dream seems too far away and too much work that they feel they don't know they are going to get from point A to that distant point B, so they give up."

"Explain," I said.

"Peep, a young homie tryna make beats might follow a producer who is already on and they see his equipment and tricked out studio and think, 'Damn, look at all that equipment he got, all I have is this old computer' and so eventually, they find a regular job and they don't lean into the dream. Or a young girl who cuts her clothes up in cool ways and is passionate about fashion and design might go online and see other women doing it big and get discouraged. All of those people never give themselves the chance, but they have the dream. And that dream is everything. That dream is a birthright. Don't undervalue your dream.

"What people don't realize is that the dream isn't the equipment, the dream isn't the fashion studio. The dream is the intangible. The dream is us right now, and us tomorrow, and us in a few months when everyone is fucking with us, and us struggling to tell our story how we want to tell it and us when we get that big check. The dream is the feeling you get when you're up late with your best friend talking about the girl you like and how she makes you feel. The dream is getting in the car with your best friend the day they get their drivers' license and you feel like you can finally go anywhere, and do anything. What I'm saying is, the dream is a trajectory achieved by those who are present for life. You are already in your dream. Us being together right now is our dream."

"But if this is the dream, why keep going?" I asked.

"You gotta meet the dream halfway, bro." Tobi took a pull of his cigarette and asked me, "What do you want, bro? What do you want so bad that if you didn't have it, nothing else would truly matter?"

He's so cool. Okay, answer his question. What do you want so bad that if you didn't have it, nothing else would really matter? I was conflicted. I wanted to say it was my family. I wanted to say it was love. I wanted to say soccer, or confidence, or millions of dollars, or validation, or success but those things weren't at the root. Someone else could control whether I had those things. I didn't want to set a goal with someone else in control of my ability to attain it.

I let his question stir. I let it move through me like a needle passing through a thread. Like a hot knife through butter. I started thinking about my old laptop in my childhood bedroom.

"A voice," I said. "I want a voice. My voice."

"How do you plan to find it?" he asked.

"Um, I guess I'll know when people start to fuck with it. Or I'll feel it."

Tobi didn't seem too impressed by that answer. He paused and looked off into the distance. "What do you want for yourself?"

Didn't I already answer that? Okay, let me think. What do I want for myself? I watched a lightning bug land on a fire hydrant. "I want to do what I want, and be able to take care of my family doing it," I finally responded.

"Okay, and what do you think you need to do to get there?"

I wanted to show Tobi that I knew myself, knew what I wanted, and had all the answers, but I didn't. I wasn't sure which way I wanted to go. I was in college for business, I had just quit the soccer team, and I felt this desire to make music. To speak to the people. To speak my mind. So I told him what I thought he wanted to hear.

"I think I need to build a following. Once I have a following, I'll be able to take that to the labels and go from there. And if I build a big enough following, I won't even need to go to the labels. I can just start my own shit and all the money will go to me," I said.

"Some people do it that way, fa sho." He paused, turned to me, and looked into my eyes. "If there was anything I could tell you, bro, it is to never stop grinding. No matter what, do not stop. Keep moving forward. Keep going."

His message was simple. So simple, in fact, I was a bit under-whelmed. *What makes him think I'm gonna stop? He think I don't live this? Were my bars not hot?* This was the first time I was insecure about my music, ever. I didn't like the feeling. It scared me. I had to respond. But what could I say to that, that wouldn't show my insecurity?

"I won't," I said. *I won't.*

THE BIKE - BROOKLYN, SPRING 2010

I wanted to go for a bike ride in NYC, and so I asked Kane if I could use his bike. Reluctantly, he let me borrow it if I promised him that nothing would happen to it. It was a glorious day. I rode through Manhattan, dipping and dodging between cars and cabs. I made my way over the Brooklyn Bridge to enjoy the sweet breeze coming off the East River.

With my headphones on, I listened to music I loved as the sun shone its beauty on my face. It was exhilarating.

After grabbing a bite to eat at a small Mexican restaurant in Williamsburg, I wanted to see if I could make it to the Brooklyn Museum before it closed. Picking up speed, I tried to bunny hop onto a curb but the back tire slammed against the curb, busting the inner tube and leaving the tire flat.

"Shit!" I grunted as I wheeled the bike off the road. *I can't tell Kane. I know what I'll do, I'll call Andy and see if he's in BK at his girl's crib to let me borrow his car.*

"Hey, Andy, you in BK?"

"Yeah, bro, what's good?"

"At your girl's crib?"

"Yeah, what's good?"

"Dope. I'm on a bike and I have a flat tire. I'm probably fifteen minutes from shorty's crib."

Andy came and picked me up. He then let me drop him off at his girl's crib and allowed me to use his car for the night. After a full night of drinking, I ended up at Cocoa's uncle's apartment in Yonkers. When I woke up, Cocoa was in the bed naked, and there was a used condom in the trash bin. When I went outside to make sure the car wasn't towed, I found the back window smashed in, and Kane's bike was gone. *Damnit, this isn't good.* I had to tell him. On my way back to the apartment building, I called Kane.

"Kane, I'm so sorry bro, I took your bike up to Yonkers and someone broke into the car and stole it," I said quickly, and vaguely.

There was silence.

"What?" Kane finally asked, aggressively.

I was taken back a bit by his response. I thought I had let him know clearly what had happened.

"Your bike was stolen, man, I'm so sorry," I reiterated.

Again, silence.

This time, the silence was heavy. The silence felt deep and personal. It felt like the silence had nothing to do with the bike, but everything to do with the bike. In the silence I could almost hear the tectonic plates shifting on the foundation of our relationship. I knew something terrible had happened the moment I saw the broken window. I knew things would be different with Kane and I from that moment forward.

WORK - ERIE, FALL 2010

24 ::beep:: Apollo checks the scanner: "Five days," he whispers.

9 ::beep:: Apollo checks the scanner: "Seven days."

17 ::beep:: Apollo checks the scanner: "Five days."

Apollo walked up and down the aisle of Hudson Hardware with the barcode gun scanning lightbulbs for inventory. As he walked, he mouthed lyrics.

"You can't touch me
Doing what you want is a life of luxury
(uh!)…You and your squad don't want war
I'm only here for a little bit, but I want more."

It had been five weeks since Apollo moved to Erie for his role at Sugar Bulb Lighting Company. He'd found himself an apartment near the zoo, and was starting to surrender to his new lifestyle. Every day looked the same. He kept his alarm set for 6:30 a.m. and woke up around 7:15. First thing he did was roll over and smoke the rest of the blunt he had left over from the night before. While his high was still fresh, he took a quick shower while he listened to the most recent underground hip-hop mixtape that was released. That week, he'd been listening to Daniel Katobi's, *A Guy Named Tobi* album.

As he was doing his usual rounds of inventory at Hudson Hardware, he got a call from his manager.

"Anthony, do you have the numbers for Hudson yet?" his manager asked in a harsh, rushed tone.

"I'm working on it now," Apollo replied lazily.

"Well, hurry up. We need those numbers, and don't miss anything again."

Miss these nuts, Apollo thought as he rolled his eyes.

Each night on his way home from work, Apollo stopped at the 76 gas station, grabbed five DutchMaster cigars, a carton of orange juice, and headed to the register where he'd see Joanna. Joanna wasn't the most conventionally attractive woman Apollo had ever met, but she was kind to him and was the closest thing he had to a friend in Erie.

"Hi, Mr. Jersey," she said. Apollo talked with her about his distaste for his job, personal struggles he'd been navigating, and his desire to work in a more creative field like media and entertainment.

"Far from home and far from finished," was her canned response to his ambitions. Sometimes she gave him a lighter for free, or a scratch-off lottery ticket someone else paid for but forgot to grab. Though they only met on Apollo's way home from work for at most five minutes, Apollo valued their discussions and Joanna did too.

After only three months on the job, Apollo got fired. He was told it was because he "showed up late and smelled like weed" too many times. Instead of getting another job doing something he didn't care about just to make some money, he decided he wanted to live his passions. His next step was to figure out what they were.

HOBOKEN, WINTER 2010

One day, I was lying in bed watching a stand-up comedy special on TV and Apollo gave me a call.

"Yo, Martin, how is school going, bro?" Apollo asked.

"It's cool, man. I quit the soccer team so I have a lot more time to work on music."

"That's deep. I see you, bro. You've really been putting in work. I'm proud of you."

"Thank you, man. It's been fun."

"I feel that," he responded in short. I could sense an awkward hesitation in his voice. His tone was as if he were feeling guilt or shame, trying to mask it with friendliness. I wanted to help, but I needed him to be transparent. I knew he was preparing for a question, but I wasn't sure what was coming.

"So, I no longer work for Sugar Bulb Lighting, that God-forsaken place, and I'm thinking of interning at Translation Marketing Agency to get my foot into that space," he started. I could sense the ask coming.

"Translation is in Manhattan, and I know your campus is right there. I was wondering if I could stay in your dormitory over the summer while I intern," he finished.

"Yeah, you can," I said.

"Wait, really? Just like that?"

"Yeah, man. I'll cut you a key. If anyone asks, just tell them you are doing research over the summer. You'll be good."

"Wow. Thank you so much, bro!" he said.

We got off the phone, and I went back to watching comedy.

PART IV:

LIFE

SWAYING - TRIBECA, SPRING 2010

The purple glare flashed across her face as she stood, leaning against the Moroccan tapestry, staring back at me—her icy blue eyes fixed on mine. I'd never seen her before, but that didn't matter. I gently ran my elbow across the bar, looking for a spot that would allow a comfortable slouch. I found it. I broke her stare. I leaned over the bar and pretended to get Tom's attention and ask for a Marty McFly, the drink they'd named after me. I was challenging her. Would she keep looking at me? Was she committed to me or was waiting on me to make the move?

I could feel the warm dry heat of her stare. I knew that sensation well. The burning desire of a woman who'd found what she was looking for. What she was waiting for. It was possible I reminded her of someone from her past. Maybe I resembled a celebrity she'd fawned over for decades. Either way, she had chosen.

She grabbed my face and pressed her tongue to my neck. I stood still. I did not freeze like a child at the sight of a loose dog but instead, like a monument. With my chin up and eyes fixed low. I stood still as if challenging her to please me. *Does she deserve me?* I knew people were looking, I didn't care. I knew that they knew I just arrived and that I did not know her. I had already won.

"Let's go," I whispered. "Jordan, let me get the keys."

In less than a minute, we were out the door. Her hands were small and soft, but firmly gripped mine. She was committed.

My eyes, barely able to adjust to the bright lights from the New York City night, darted across the street to the MDX. The clicking of her heels behind me was like cans on a string tied to the bride and groom's vehicle as they strode away in matrimony. We weren't quite as honorable, though we were both ready for a journey we had never taken. She had won me for the moment. How long that moment lasted was up to how well she pleased me. I never looked back at her on the way to the MDX, but I could feel her gaze on the left side of my face. She loved me, and I had never gotten her name.

ENID'S PRAYER - FRANKLIN, SPRING 2010

"Father God, I ask that you watch over my sweet son, Father God. As he goes out into the world to do your blessing, Father God. I pray that you expand his territory, Father God. May your love for him be big. May your love for him be mighty, Father God. May your angels guide him each and every step of the way, Father God. May their love for him be mighty and big, Father God. May they be with him at every corner, at every turn, ever with him, Father God. May he be guided by giants of your glory, Father God. May he be outside with elephants, Father God. In your name, I thank you. Father God, I thank you for your love, for your blessings and for your grace. Father God, I lift you up and I praise you. In your name, I pray. Amen." Enid said.

My mother then blew out the candles and rested her head on her pillow, staring out the window, thinking of her boy.

TRANSLATION, WINTER 2010

The first night in the dormitory for Apollo was challenging. He was grateful, but uncertain about his future and whether he'd made the right decision. *Am I bugging? What am I doing here? Nah, this is the step I need to take to get to where I'm trying to go. This is bravery.* His internal dialogue was conflicted.

As he laid his head to go to sleep in preparation for his first day on the job, he heard a noise. He shut off the light, leaned off the bed, and looked into the darkness in the direction of the sound. His eyes had not yet adjusted to the blackness of the room. As he peered over the bed, his head and his shoulders off the edge, the rest of his body remained under the covers. He held still for a moment. His eyes and ears scanned along the bottom of the wall closest to him. His eyes met the crack under the only door in the room. A faint light could be seen coming from an open door down the hall.

Nothing.

He decided it was alright and began to lean back, debating whether to keep his socks on or kick them off. He chose to keep them on because he wasn't sure if the air conditioning running through the dormitory was on auto or if it would be running through the night.

THE STRUGGLE - HOBOKEN/MANHATTAN, WINTER 2010/SPRING 2011

Apollo's days were, again, beginning to all look the same. He'd wake up, walk to the train with very little money, and struggle to make ends meet, all while living in my dormitory. Until one day, eight weeks from his start date, he came back into my room smiling. I was at my computer desk eating a slice of pizza, trying to figure out how to approach an instrumental a friend sent me.

"Bro, I got the job," Apollo said, surprised.

"Yeah?" I replied.

"Yeah, man. You are now looking at a Marketing Associate for Translation Agency."

Apollo didn't sound so excited. In fact, he sounded a bit sad.

"That's amazing, bro. I didn't even know you were interviewing."

"After the internship, they gave a few of us roles, and I got one."

"Then why do you sound so sad?" I asked.

"You know, Marty. Sometimes, when you want something so bad, and you get it, it's hard to celebrate because you know it's never the end." He cleared his throat. "Where I'm headed? Heaven only knows, bro. But today is a good day."

"Respect, bro. Congrats," I said as I opened the pizza box to grab another slice.

THE BREWERY - BROOKLYN, SUMMER 2012

After the success of Tobi's *Sleepless Nights* and *A Guy Named Tobi: The Album*, Dez had made a great deal of money. He was one of the three main producers on Tobi's projects, and that earned him a pretty penny. Instead of spending all his money on cars and clothes like a lot of his peers, he bought out a loft space in Brooklyn and built a state-of-the-art music recording studio. Because of my connection with Tobi, through Lisa, Dez's Studio in Brooklyn had become my home base. Whenever it was time to lay down something I was confident in, I went to his space—The Brewery.

One day I walked into the studio with weed, a flask of Jameson, and some cocaine. I went into the bathroom, snorted a few bumps off my keys, and headed back out into the common area. My heart was racing. My phone was flooded with texts from friends letting me know they were in Brooklyn and would be coming to the session. First three people showed up, then five, then ten. Jordan came out. Apollo was there, V, Kane, Ceza, Uche: everyone. Soon, it was a performance. I didn't care. I knew I had a song to make, and I needed to get into my zone. *Coke, weed, Jameson. I'll be good.*

After shaking a few hands, I walked into the booth.

"From the top," I demanded.

The live room grew still. Everyone's eyes were on me.

"People making promises, I ain't waiting for it
Start speaking your mind and they'll hate you for it
Starting acting a fool and they'll make you for it
And they think you'll do whatever if they pay you for it
What you take me for?
I ain't dumb
Ridin' round the city with my finger on a gun
Paranoia sticking like a splinter through a thumb
So much pain inside my brain, I'd rather take what keeps
me numb."

When I walked out of the studio, I entered the live room to full applause. It sounded like I had scored the game-winning goal, but all I could think about was when I could sneak away for the next bump. *Can they tell? Fuck it, I'm going to the bathroom.*

CRUSHED - TRIBECA, FALL 2012

When Carmen walked into Sway, he was mobbed by friends. After shaking hands and hugging some girls, he led me to the front bar to get us drinks from the bartender, Tom.

"Tom! What's good, you beautiful mother fucker you!"

"Hey, Carmen! How are ya?"

"I'm really good, you know, just here with some friends. Can I have three Jameson's on the rocks when you have a chance?"

"You got it."

Tom handed Carmen the glasses. He didn't wait for Carmen to pay, he just gave them to him and moved on. Carmen tipped him twenty dollars, then turned and handed me a shot glass.

"Cheers, my friend, to the future! This is our city. This is to us, to all of us. I love you, let's get it!"

"Let's get it," I repeated as I threw the shot down the hatchet.

"Let's go to the back," Carmen said. "It's chiller back there."

Carmen always had this way about him, where he could be very present with you but was also intensely aware of his surroundings. Walking behind him, I noticed his head always on a swivel, always knowing who was where and what that meant to the space. His relationship with space and time was artistic. Where I made music, he made community. He was an incredible connector of people.

On our way to the back bar, he leaned in to tell me something that felt like a secret.

"Bro, I'm in love," he said.

I looked around. "Which one?"

"No, nobody here. I'm in love, man. Like, It's crazy," Carmen repeated. "I've never felt this strongly about someone. She's traveled to London, Brazil, Tokyo, all over the world for fashion, man. She's incredible. When I look at her, it just feels right. Her style, her mind, it's all incredible, bro."

Wow. He's really digging this girl.

For a moment, I began to get excited about this person. For Carmen to love someone the way he said he did, she must be something else.

"That's what's up, man," I said. "I'm happy for you."

"Her name is Debra, and she is landing at JFK tonight at midnight. I'm gonna head up to the Bronx to this party in a little bit. Do you think you could get her from the airport?"

"JFK? And then do what? Go to the Bronx?"

"Yeah, bro. I'll be at Turu's. You just come through with Debra."

I hated the sound of that. John F. Kennedy International Airport and the Bronx were fifty minutes to an hour apart on a good night. Realistically, I wouldn't make it to the Bronx until 2 a.m. at the earliest. I also felt a bit slighted, like I was some sort of runner or child. At the same time, I wanted to be in Carmen's good graces, and to do him a favor like this would show my loyalty to him. Naturally, I conceded.

I left Sway promptly and arrived at JFK airport around midnight to pick Debra up. I had only seen photos of her online, and wasn't sure to expect. I waited outside the terminal for no more than three minutes when she came walking out of the terminal.

She looks smaller than I imagined. She walked up to the car, shyly.

"Hey! Are you Marty?"

"Yeah."

"Whew! Cool! I was afraid to ask. Hello! It's so nice to meet you! Carmen has told me so much about you."

"Same," I replied with an unfamiliar excitement. My heart began to beat faster. *She's...shy.*

I quickly got out of the car and gently placed her bag in the trunk. She got into the passenger seat, and we drove off. When she stepped into the car, I felt it. It was heavy. Something unspoken. A heat that was familiar to me. *Wait. Does she like me?*

I didn't want what I was feeling to be true, though it felt good. I felt accepted. I felt seen. Our mouths hadn't said much since getting in the car, but we were loud. I couldn't hear myself think, but I could hear her think. *Can she hear me?* I asked her about her trip, but we both didn't care.

The only thing that mattered was that she was there and that we were there together. We were shy, and we were young, and we didn't really understand what was happening. It was beautifully awkward, and I hated her for it. I despised her for putting this wedge between Carmen and me. I despised her for seeing me. I despised how gentle she was. I despised how delicate she was. I despised that this was how it was to be.

With my hands on the steering wheel, I could see the lights of Manhattan in the distance. The city skyline always looked the same to me, as if the same lights in the same windows were always on. I knew at that moment, the beginning of the end had arrived. I stepped on the gas and switched lanes to avoid a slowing vehicle with its hazards on. Debra looked at me briefly and looked away before I could return the gaze. I rolled my window down, never taking my eyes off the road as the city loomed closer and closer.

APOLLO GETS INTERVIEWED - LOS ANGELES, SPRING 2013

"What's good, world? You know what time it is. You got me, Dupri, the lovely Laura, and you got Mr. Rosenthal. Today on the show, we have our man Anthony "Apollo" Apollon. Give it up for my man! You may see him on *Culture and Now* and his award-winning *The Ground Up* podcast."

Apollo shifted in his seat a bit. "What's up, y'all? Incredible to be on the show today. Thank you for having me."

"Absolutely. Thank you for joining us. You've been super busy, man. *Culture and Now*, *The Ground Up* podcast. Rumors are you're working on your own shoe. What's up, dude?"

"Yeah, thank you. Um, I been doing all that, haha. It's been special. It's been a long road, and there's a lot more I want to do. A lot more I want to share with the culture." Apollo took a sip of water out of a glass the studio had provided to him. He took a long look at the glass. It was a crystal *Biricolli* glass made from sand off the Amalfi coast. *They had this here, for me. I've come a long way, man.*

"What about you as a person led you to this path? You are one of the few who really care about what you're doing. Why did you choose that?"

"I don't know. I guess I was raised right. When I started in this industry, I came up under Sasha Jenkins and Timmy Listermann. At Translation, it was Dan Rimpy, Nigel Jones, Brendan Fredricks, Drew Quail. I'm also a magazine kid. I listened to hip-hop radio every morning. New mixtapes every morning. You get steered. And I think if you got diverted to social media or where the clout is, you'll do that. That's not my thing."

"What do you have to say for anyone who wants to follow in your footsteps?"

"I say, if you are next to Rosenthal and you feel like you can't keep up, that feeling inside that you feel should shake you. And you should be like, 'Let me keep up.' Let that moment serve as a realization that you have more work to do. You've got to work at your craft the point that you can't let them shake you. Listen, man, I've been embarrassed, I've done the wrong thing, and I've made mistakes but then put my head down and did the work. Now I'm here." Apollo grabbed the glass again. It was almost empty. He looked around and noticed a studio hand looking directly at him with a shy smile in his eyes. Apollo gave him a head nod, and the studio hand quickly walked over with a bottle of water. *Wow.*

"How do you feel about where you are now?"

"Man, I feel good but I'm a bit—I'm at this dangerous place, where I feel like I have all the answers. You know, sometimes the people you've been reaching out to are not the ones who are responding in the way that you want. Then what? Reach out to other people. And then the other people will come around to your ideas.

"It's constantly having to get outside of your box and your own way. Keep your own personal momentum up.

"For instance, I'll get busy with my real life or get a 'No' and that'll like, take me out the game for a little bit and needing to have the momentum or I'll start thinking about how many kids on the internet that are like, 'Yo, I just want to work.' I find that funny because sometimes it's just bullshit. A lot of people don't want to do the work. I'm extremely judgmental about that stuff. I think at the end of the day, you know who's real, who wants to do the work. Motherfuckers want to throw themselves a parade. but who actually wants to go through the trenches and put feet to the pavement is the real question."

"It couldn't have been easy to make that change," the radio host offered.

"It isn't something I've thought about too much. I'm not like, 'Oh, man, I should go do some other thing.' In fact, people offered me jobs over time but I'm like, 'Oh, that's not really what I want' or, learning about myself and being like, 'Why did these other situations not necessarily work for me?' I started to realize that I like a ton of control. I like a ton of control over what I'm saying, where I'm at, who I'm going to surround myself with—and the same goes for all of my content. Now I'm realizing my levels outside of that like not only just what time of the day I wake up, but I want control of the whole shit. I need it."

"How do you think got to where you are?"

"I'm in this because I had an appreciation. I'm in this because Dan and Nigel said they were putting together a magazine in the other room and I walked over there. I'm here because someone was like 'Yo, I'm working at this brand,' and I had respect for the brand so I went over there. I'm here because I fought to get to an ad agency and was like, 'Yo, I love these commercials, I love these music videos I want to be over here.' I was reminded recently that I am in this space because I actually respect and appreciate it. I deserve to put my two cents in. I'm real about it."

"Any last words for our listeners?"

"Do what moves you. If it doesn't move you, move."

OVER

I wish I could say I told Carmen how Debra and I felt about each other, but I didn't. Instead, I started a romantic relationship with her behind his back. He didn't find out until I sent him a text that I meant to send to her saying: *He is leaving now, come over.*

He knew who it was for. From that moment on, my relationship with Carmen soured. He no longer supported my music career, and we no longer spent time together.

Debra and I ended up dating for four years. Between 2013 and 2016, my drug and alcohol abuse worsened and by the summer of 2016, I couldn't go out without a pack of cigarettes, a bag of weed, and some cocaine. Eventually, Debra left me. That was when things got really bad. The guilt and shame became so strong that I spiraled out of control. I was doing drugs every night, all night. I wasn't eating, I wasn't sleeping, and I wasn't taking care of myself. I had gotten fired from my job as a youth soccer coach, and I was cash poor and in deep debt. Until one day in early 2016, Lisa called me.

"Hey, Marty? How are you? It's been a while," she started.

I rolled over and covered my eyes from the sunlight shining in through my bedroom windows. My head was throbbing from lack of sleep. I'd been up all night drinking and doing drugs with people at a local bar.

"I'm okay, Lisa. What's up?" I replied, voice trembling.

"Honestly, I'm a little concerned about you, Marty."

I rubbed my eyes. My body was unable to release any chemical other than cortisol. I began feverishly twirling my hair. "What's up, Lisa?"

She sighed. "I'm hearing things about you, Marty. People are saying they are seeing you out, and you aren't looking good and you're saying crazy things. Please, just hear me out. A friend of mine goes to this thing every year. It's a ten-day silent meditation retreat in California. I want to send you. I want you to go. Will you go?"

I was in pain. My head hurt. My body felt weak. I had lost at least fifteen pounds from the substance abuse. I was desperate for intervention.

"Yes," I said, surrendering.

She let out a deep sigh of relief. "Okay, Marty. I'm buying your ticket now. I'll call you tomorrow."

"Alright, Lisa."

"Alright, Marty. Get some rest."

"Okay, Lisa, Bye."

"Bye."

APOLLO INTERVIEWS TOBI - MANHATTAN, FEBRUARY 2016

Tobi arrived at REVOLT studios wearing a pair of ripped denim jeans, a long ripped white t-shirt, and a black leather jacket. He had just come supermodel Becky McCollum's apartment not far from REVOLT studios in Soho. He and Becky had been watching their favorite movie, *Amélie*.

When Tobi arrived, Apollo was sorting through his notes. Apollo was nervous. He was a huge Tobi fan, and finally had the opportunity to interview him.

"Tobi, so good to have you here, bro, how are you?"

"I'm good, man, working on a new project, which is always exciting."

"Not just for you, man, we've all been waiting on something new from you. What inspired this new project?" Apollo asked, hands trembling.

"Honestly, the same thing that inspires them all. Love. Being there for myself. Fighting my demons. It never changes, man. I'm here to do one thing and that is save lives."

Tobi had a look at his watch. *9:46 p.m.* He was slotted to be in the studio with Tunji at 10 p.m. *I'm gonna be late...Whatever... This is important.* Apollo noticed when Tobi looked at his watch but was relieved when Tobi didn't show any anxiety. He exhaled deeply in relief. *This is important to him, too.*

"You used to work with Simple Sam. He was an integral part of Tunji's team and then your team. Is that relationship still there?"

"Absolutely, Sam will always be on my team. He's a big brother to me. You know, when I was coming up, there weren't too many people believing in me. It was Sam. Now all these motherfuckers wanna pretend like they been down for me the whole time. Nah. It was Dez and Sam from jump, and we made the music we wanted to make, and the kids needed it. I needed it, that why I made it."

"Right, I remember, after the success of *Sleepless Nights* and then having worked with Tunji on his record-breaking album *We All Knew*, it seemed like it all happened pretty fast for you. What was that like?"

Tobi shifted in his seat, and a cold deep gaze ran across his face. Apollo felt Tobi's reaction and knew it was a good question. He leaned forward.

"It was crazy. Man, a lot of people don't know this, but it was hard. You know, I actually turned to drugs. I was doing a lot of coke, you know. By myself to just deal. I would go out on the street, throw my shades on, and I was just on coke saying what's up to the fans. Tryna cope."

Tobi's eyes were on Apollo, but it was as if he was looking through him.

"I came up with a lot of folk in New York at that time, and I was the only one with money. You know, I had money then for the first time, and that's a challenge when you feel like you're leaving everyone behind. It was bittersweet, man."

"Thank you for sharing that. That is an interesting perspective. I'm sure a lot of people watching this would think that it was all good, and all sweet but there were places where you struggled," Apollo said

Tobi took a sip of water. "The struggle was real, in many ways. I moved out to New York with nothing. My uncle took me in, and I couldn't pay him rent so I left and stayed with Dez. Dez held me down in a way I will never forget. When we lived together, Dez and I worked on songs day and night, and *Sleepless Nights* was born. The rest is history, bro. But it was hard. There was a lot of pain at that time."

"What do you do with that pain?"

"Damn, I never got that question before. Sometimes I kick things. I'm playing, but really, music is therapeutic for me, so I take it there. It's a place I can go when I don't know what else to do. I think the key is to allow yourself to experience what you are feeling without judgment. Then observe the experience deeply. The better I can understand my pain, the more authentic and potent my message and my storytelling. The more potent my storytelling, the more positive an impact I can have on these kids. On these lives."

"Right, and that is super evident in your music. I'm curious, what do you want to be remembered for when you die?"

"Man, it isn't about me being remembered. It's about the message; and the message is simple. Never give up. Never stop fighting. Keep moving forward and you will arrive."

"Do you feel like you have arrived?"

"I think arriving is different for everyone. Musically, have I arrived? Check me out, bro. My goal was super clear from the beginning. From the moment I found my voice, my goal has been to get my message to as many people as possible. I was going into label meetings just to spread the word, 'bout ready to sign my life away for my message. But arriving in general? Every time I show up for myself, I feel like I've arrived. Every time my heart is broken, and I create that space for myself to feel that. I arrived. It's work though, bro. And work I can't ever stop doing."

"Tobi, thank you for your time. It was an absolute pleasure. I look forward to hearing the album!"

"Thank you for having me, bro. Nice to meet you, man. I respect you and how you do what you do. I can imagine you had to climb some mountains to get where you are as well."

Apollo's eyes widened and stung. "Thank you, Tobi. That means a lot. And yeah, I had some mountains to climb, but I had a few Dez's in my life as well. We need them."

"A hundred percent, man. Be good, bro." Tobi shook Apollo's hand and exited the studio.

VIPASSANA (FEBRUARY 2016)

DAY 1 – ARRIVAL

"This is my first time," I said, as I handed the pale young woman my phone. The North Folk Vipassana Meditation Center stood about twenty yards off a windy road in Kelseyville, California. The distinct smell of redwood filled the air, unescapable and humble. Cars pulled up, unloading strangers with colorful hiking bags, sleeping backs, canteens, pillows, and headlamps. All I had was the clothes on my back and a backpack stuffed with a pillow, two pairs of boxer briefs, a towel, and another pair of socks.

"You can go to your room and put your things down and relax. Our first group sit will be at 8 p.m.," the pale young woman at the table told me.

"Thank you."

This is going to be long. Will I be attracted to anyone here? Let's see. Let's have a look at the schedule.

4:00 a.m.: Wake-up Bell.
4:30 a.m. — 6:30 a.m.: Meditate.
6:30 a.m. — 8:00 a.m.: Breakfast.
8:00 a.m. — 11:00 a.m.: Meditate.
11:00 a.m. — 1:00 p.m.: Lunch.
1:00 p.m. — 5:00 p.m.: Meditate.
5:00p.m. — 6:00 p.m.: Tea.
6:00 p.m. — 7:00 p.m.: Meditate.

Wow, that is a lot of meditating. But that's good. Yeah, that will be good for me. Hm…I wonder how many black people are here. I saw the one lady and the one guy with the orange… Okay, so…No talking, No journaling, no eye contact. I'm with that. Man, I literally have no money. How will I get back to New York? All good…God got me. Surrender to the experience. Surrender to the experience. Surrender to the experience. Breathe.

Upon arriving in my room, I put down my backpack and set up my bed. It was just going to be me this week. Though I was scared, I was excited. I was happy. Deep down, I knew that I was beginning a necessary journey.

I'd lied. I'd cheated. I'd stolen. I'd messed up. It was time to reconcile my differences with myself, and I finally had gotten away from the danger zone. I was safe to heal.

After putting down my backpack, I left the room to walk the grounds and explore. About twenty yards away from the front door of the cabin was a park bench facing a meadow. I walked toward the park bench slowly, keeping my eyes on the meadow. A cloud was rolling into the mountain, and the sun was a few moments from setting. Staring into the distance, I thought of Bianca. I thought of Carmen, and I thought of my old laptop.

DAY 2

The morning bell sounded at 4 a.m. *Mph, Okay.* I didn't have much trouble getting out of bed—I was anxious like a child the night before Christmas or the first day of school. I sat up and gently removed the sheets from my legs. *I am here to slow down.* The room was dark, but I could faintly see the shadow of my roommate moving in the distance. Based on the consistency of the sound coming from his direction, he was getting up as well. *Take a shower.* I crossed my legs and took a few deep breaths. I was no longer hungry, no longer scared. No one here knew me or knew anything about what I had done. That gave me hope. All my troubles were in New York, and I wasn't.

After the shower, I walked back into my room. My roommate was gone. I put on the only clothes I had. My cargo pants, t-shirt, turtleneck, lumberjack flannel, and scarf. Outside was chilly. I noticed the stars, the trees, and the lights on the side of other cabins that made the shadows of the early morning look like dancing figures in the distance.

I arrived at the meditation hall to find the room sparse. I was nervous. This was the beginning of something new. Something slow. I had spent so much time moving fast and thinking that the faster I moved, the more successful I was. And now, I was deliberately moving slow. It was already challenging, and I had only been there for ten hours.

First full day. Surrender to the experience. I'm a bit tired. Okay so, one hour then a five-minute break and then another hour. I can do this. My mind was racing. *It's so calm in here. What is my sister doing right now? My mom? My mom.*

Tears began to roll down my face. *My mom loves me so much. Thank you, God, for this experience. Please allow me to surrender to this and get closer to you. I am here, and I will be present.*

I gently lowered my body onto the pillow I'd been assigned. *This is my pillow.*

Be here. Be here.

DAY 7

At breakfast on day seven, I had an epiphany. *What was that thing I loved, before I knew what love was? Soccer. Okay, how can I use soccer to provide opportunities to others? Wait, first I need to decide who I want to support with soccer. Young black kids? Be more specific. Incredibly underprivileged youth. But who? Immigrant youth? Refugee youth? What are they seeking refuge from? Ah, that's not the important piece. Okay, using soccer to support immigrant and refugee youth. Wow, okay. Where will I do that? How will I do that?*

I slowly grabbed my spoon, inhaling as I brought it closer to me and exhaling as I held it over my oatmeal. In my peripheral view, I noticed a gentleman meditating over his food. I am not sure why, but I felt drawn to this gentleman in the moment. He had light brown hair, tanned white skin, and a scruffy beard. I'd seen him around since day one. There were only thirty men on site and—though we could not talk to each other or communicate in any way during the retreat—I somehow felt like I knew him. He looked so peaceful. Like a child. That resonated with me because I felt like a child, too. I did not try to get his attention or to throw any energy his way, but I saw him. In that moment I saw him, and it brought me peace.

DAY 11

The morning of the eleventh day was glorious. It was the first time we were able to speak after ten long days of silence, meditating, walking, using the bathroom, and sleeping. All retreat participants wasted no time in getting to know each other. As I walked up to the lunch cabin where everyone was congregating, I began to cry. There was something so sacred about our silence. I didn't want it to end. I was safe in the silence, and that safety was being ripped from me. I was going to have to go back to life. I was scared.

I was just about to turn and go back to my dorm to meditate when I saw the brown-haired, bearded gentleman I had noticed at lunch that day.

"Hey!" he shouted in the distance.

"Hey, how's it going?" I asked as we walked toward one another.

"Good! It's interesting to hear what you sound like!" he said playfully.

I laughed to be nice. I knew he noticed the sadness in me. I could feel him sensing it.

He changed his tone. "It's tough breaking the silence."

"It is," I confirmed.

"The last ten days were a great gift to give to ourselves, and now, use what we've learned to move humanity forward," he said.

"Hmph. Yeah, I guess so."

"My name is Ted. It's really nice to meet you."

"My name is Martin, and it's nice to meet you too."

We were just about to part when I stopped him. "Hey, Ted, when you go back to wherever you are going, what are you going back to?"

He stopped and turned. "An organization I founded called *Futbol Without Boundaries*. We support immigrant, refugee, and asylum-seeking youth using soccer as a vehicle for positive change."

I looked at Ted. I noticed how gentle his eyes were. And how impossibly blue. I thought of Ms. Connie in the driveway those many years before. I thought

"That sounds really cool, Ted," I said. "Could you use a volunteer?"

Ted turned and flashed a gentle smile.

"Sure. But your office would be outside."

We laughed together.

"That's perfect," I replied.

End

Made in the USA
Middletown, DE
01 September 2020

17046042R00086